TRIGGER

ALSO BY N. GRIFFIN

The Whole Stupid Way We Are
Just Wreck It All

N. GRIFFIN

TRIGGER

atheneum

NEW YORK   LONDON   TORONTO
SYDNEY   NEW DELHI

A CAITLYN DLOUHY BOOK

atheneum

An imprint of Simon & Schuster Children's Publishing Division
1230 Avenue of the Americas, New York, New York 10020
For information about special discounts for bulk purchases, please contact Simon & Schuster Special Sales at 1-866-506-1949 or business@simonandschuster.com.
The Simon & Schuster Speakers Bureau can bring authors to your live event. For more information or to book an event, contact the Simon & Schuster Speakers Bureau at 1-866-248-3049 or visit our website at www.simonspeakers.com.
The text for this book was set in ITC New Baskerville Std.
Manufactured in the United States of America
First Edition
10 9 8 7 6 5 4 3 2 1
Library of Congress Cataloging-in-Publication Data
Names: Griffin, N., author.
Title: Trigger / N. Griffin.
Description: First edition. | New York : Atheneum, an imprint of Simon & Schuster Children's Publishing Division, [2022] | "A Caitlyn Dlouhy Book." | Audience: Ages 12 up. | Audience: Grades 7–9. | Summary: Didi's father is constantly pressuring her to do better: win at chess, run faster every day, shoot better, hunt better or go hungry; she is not allowed friends, or time off or any pleasures; he always reminds her that they have to be prepared to fight the rest of the world—but what he never tells her is that when she is the best he plans to hunt her.
Identifiers: LCCN 2021018955 (print) | LCCN 2021018956 (ebook) | ISBN 9781534487178 (hardcover) | ISBN 9781534487185 (paperback) | ISBN 9781534487192 (ebook)
Subjects: LCSH: Psychologically abused children—Juvenile fiction. | Psychological torture—Juvenile fiction. | Fathers and daughters—Juvenile fiction. | Survivalism—Juvenile fiction. | Psychology, Pathological—Juvenile fiction. | Young adult fiction. | CYAC: Psychological abuse—Fiction. | Fathers and daughters—Fiction. | Survivalism—Fiction. | Mental illness—Fiction. | LCGFT: Psychological fiction. | Thrillers (Fiction)
Classification: LCC PZ7.G88135934 Tr 2022 (print) | LCC PZ7.G88135934 (ebook) | DDC 813.6 [Fic]—dc23
LC record available at https://lccn.loc.gov/2021018955
LC ebook record available at https://lccn.loc.gov/2021018956

FOR BREE

Running. Running.

Pounding fast through the grass. Slamming the ground with every step—

Shut up!

Anybody could hear her and Didi wasn't dealing with an anybody.

No idea where to look, no idea where to go, bullet bigger than a chess pawn waiting for her neck.

Slideslipping down, down, down the path and into the field.

Get ready, get ready, get ready, get rea—

Running body, taut and lean—Didi didn't know what was coming.

Or actually—

she did.

PART 1

DIDI: AGED FIFTEEN

HUNT

"MOVE!"

Didi's dad ripped the covers off her. Didi quickly whipped her legs down and around the edge of the couch where she slept.

"Get dressed. Now."

All she had on were the T-shirt and shorts she slept in—where was her camo?

Oh—

—last night changing in the bathroom—it was in there, folded on top of the towels. She better get in the bathroom fast before he—

"Didi! What the hell is taking so long?"

The bathroom door jerked open and there was her dad. But she already had the shirt over her head and down and was pulling up the pants.

"Out. Now. We're going to hunt."

Canteens filled. Shotguns out. Combat boots for him, sneakers on Didi. The sneakers got soaked quickly from frost outside, so her feet were freezing, but that didn't matter. What did?

Bag a deer in one.

That did.

"I got this," she told her dad. They were out and slipstepping down the wet grassy slope behind the ridge at the yard's edge. Open fields stretched out down here, rimmed by a forest full of evergreens and oaks that wound back up and around her dad's property. The October morning was still gray in the dawn, sun not yet up over the ridge to warm it with its pale fall light. Too early in the year for legal hunting season, but that never mattered. They needed meat, and it was in his fields for free.

Quiet now.

Slow steps.

Crouching down low.

What was that?

Over there. A group of delicate shapes.

One white-tailed deer standing apart from her sisters at the littoral of field and wood.

BOOM.
SHOT.

Impact. Didi got her in one.

"Excellent," said her dad, moving forward. "Come on. We need to bag the meat before you go to school."

Little rabbit in the wood

RACE

BOOM!
 SHOT!
The PE teacher's start gun went and Didi was off and flying in the small pack of eleventh graders running the mile in the intrasquad meet. The day was unusually freezing with wild red foliage surrounding the track and athletic fields. Didi was in shorts anyway, because what else was she going to wear, the camo? Her sneakers were still damp from the morning hunt but there was no time to think about that because

focus!

Didi was in it to win.

The track was edged with the juniors not running this race, some of her fellow chess club members among them. Pascal, Oscar and Dallin were the loudest to cheer Didi on, excited to see one of their own exhibit physical capabilities.

"Go, Didi!"

"You're amazing!"

"Get up, get up, get *up*!" from the gym teacher, who always wanted Didi to beat her own record time.

Didi sprinted easily ahead of the small pack of runners, practically leaping over some of them like a knight on a chessboard. On and on she sprinted. In real life, Didi could run in a near sprint practically forever. But no one else knew that. They just knew they wanted Didi on their team for anything fast. For any sport, really, but her speed was what was useful for today.

No one had a chance to catch her. Didi lapped some of the slowest who lagged behind the pack, kids who did not care in the least about this race and were just jogging slowly along, talking about clothes.

The finish line was up ahead. Red-pinnied teammates waiting for her, screaming her name. Faster sprint for the end of such a short run—

She heaved her chest forward, and it was done.

"Four thirty-nine! Fantastic time!" screamed the PE teacher.

Fantastic? Not really. Maybe for their teeny rural Carthage Town school, but Didi knew she'd have way more competition somewhere else.

Still, the PE teacher moved to slap her on the back. Didi was too quick for her and shifted away. The teacher dropped her hand and shook her head. "Why you won't join cross country or track is beyond me," she began, but Didi was already angling away from the red-team people coming at her—

"Great job, Didi!"

"You are so damn fast!"

Oh God, Dallin squirming forward to hug her—

Didi backed up and away from them and they raised their hands to slap hers with congratulations.

Back up. Back up.

Didi backed up faster and faster until she could turn and jog away. Jogging, jogging, and then she was running, away from the team, the track and the fields. She ran as fast as she could toward the locker room. PE was pretty much over anyway. Advanced Calc was next. *Test in there today.* Didi knew she better be the best with that, too. To the locker room, then, to get dressed.

Though what she really wanted was to keep running right now, fast past the school and the single road of this nothing town. Up, up, up and out until she was gone, was flying, was free.

CHESS

There are a lot of pieces on a chessboard and they move in all different ways. The knight goes two up or over and then one in another direction to make an L, oriented in any fashion. The bishop moves diagonally, as far or as near as they want. And the queen. Queen, queen of the land. She can move in whatever direction she likes. Forward, to the side, diagonally if she wants. Different for the pawns, though. After their first move from their line that protects the big pieces, when they're allowed to move two squares ahead, pawns can only move one square. And only forward.

Actually, it's all a little more complicated than this, but that's enough for now.

Didi, do you want me to—

Quick stride fast, as fast as she could run.

Crash, trip, stumble back up—Didi ran toward the far edge of the field. Trees rimmed its border, evergreens mostly, but also some beech with their leaves shaped like pears. Above her, unbelievably, birds were singing. Robins and sparrows, unmindful of her desperation below.

What do you care about robins and pears?! Focus!

Oh God, why had she run to this field? Leaving her offense open with no defense to speak of? Who knew who was behind her, getting closer and closer?

But Didi's feet remembered and she ran.

PART 2

DIDI: AGED FIVE

TAUGHT

When her dad was out overnight for supplies, Didi got up early, early, early, hopped into clothes and ran outside around her dad's property three times, as fast as she could, which to be honest wasn't fast enough. But Didi was trying. His property was big and part of it snaked into the woods. Didi made herself run in there too, even though a bear had snuck out of those trees once. He was looking for things to eat and Didi was scared of the bear because what if he forgot he liked nuts and berries and decided he liked Didi instead?

But no bear came out today. Last lap run, heart pounding and breathing hard, Didi plopped down on the ground at the edge of the long, stony backyard, right on the ridge over the valley. This early morning was full of birds in the trees and some fog down below, looking like a cloud that fell down. But the sun was shining above her, working to burn that fog away.

Chipmunks skittered in the stones. Bluebirds chirped and also robins—good, loud chirping to show how strong they were. There weren't any fresh nests, though. Robin nests were long empty, now that it was fall. Pops of blue in the nests in the eaves and trees, beautiful blue eggs, and then baby birds with gawping mouths for feeding—that was in the spring.

The chipmunks were fat and cute.

Didi's stomach rumbled. She wouldn't mind having some breakfast, but she thought it would be better to wait for her dad and eat with him. She didn't have a mom anymore, like some other kids did. Where was she? Didi didn't know. Brown hair and a long soft sweater. Face as foggy as the valley below.

Maybe she does a secret job and has to be in a disguise, thought Didi. *Maybe that's why she doesn't come be here.*

She hoped her dad would bring home some Lucky Charms with the supplies he was out buying. Didi loved Lucky Charms and played games with the charms in her overfilled bowl. She chased the moon around with her spoon, so it stood just above the rainbow, and then she stuck the clover underneath the rainbow. That was the right way for those three charms to be: How could a clover possibly float higher than the moon? Didi's favorites were the stars, and she pushed them over to the edge of her bowl soaring over the rainbow and moon. She knew she should make the stars be farther away than she put them, but it wasn't possible in just a cereal bowl. When her dad wasn't home, she took the damp stars completely out of the bowl and arranged them at the far end of the kitchen table to show more better where they should actually be.

The hearts and the horseshoes and the hourglasses, though. She was never sure where to put those, so she usually just picked them out and ate them one by one. The balloons, she let float in the milk.

Thinking about those charms made her stomach rumble again. She smooshed it in and thought

No.

No cereal yet. Besides, they didn't even have any Lucky Charms left.

So Didi sat on the ridge and listened to the birds. She tried to mimic what she heard. She was pretty good at sounding like a robin—*cheerily-cheer-up-cheer-up-cheerily-cheer-up!* Didi wasn't trying to trick the robins. She just wanted to learn their song so she could pretend to be one sometimes and play that she was flying across the valley. She had to be muscly and strong because flying looked hard, but then she'd be able to go where she wanted, like a grown-up, if she played Robin. Sometimes she practiced chipmunk sounds too, but they were harder to do, with more clucks and chirrups. The good thing about playing chipmunk was that you could pretend to squeeze into cozy spaces and stay warm and hidden, even in the sun.

little rabbit in the wood

The warmth from running had left Didi's body now, and her jacket was still in the house. She wanted it even though it was so small that she couldn't really get all the way in it anymore.

I'm cold. I'm going in to read. Didi couldn't remember the name of her book, but the story was about a puzzle and some clues. She went inside the house and into the living room with its scratchy wooden walls. Lying on the windowsill, she

read and laughed at the funny parts of her book until . . .
RRRRROOOOOM.

Didi snapped her head up. That was truck noise. Her dad was home. She better go help and make it fast. But her dad was through the door and into the living room with a box in his arms before Didi could wheel her feet to the floor.

Her father wasn't mad, though. *Phew.*

"What're you reading, Didi Read-ie?" he rhymed, and she held up the book.

"It's my favorite forever now," she said. "It's about a mystery that people have to solve to find this guy."

"Huh," said her father, but she knew he was thinking about the supplies in the truck. She was right. "Come on. There's stuff to unload."

"Sure thing," said Didi, and she shoved the book under the couch and speedy-walked outside again, following her dad. The truck was full of things from the hardware store, mostly, but Didi spotted some new Lucky Charms right away. Plus her dad was happy this morning. Didi already loved the day.

She picked up the boxes her dad set on the ground and ferried them into the kitchen. Didi was a strong little thing, her dad said, and Didi knew he liked that. Even if her running was still slower than he wanted it to be. It was his idea that she run laps around the property when she woke up, to get better. Didi agreed. She was sick of being so slow.

"All right," said her dad now. "Good job with the carrying."

Didi stared at her feet and swallowed her smile. Then she

looked up at her dad's face. "Are we going to unpack the boxes now too?" Her book was waiting under the window.

"I'll unload later, by myself," said her father. "There are things in those boxes that are just for me. But," he continued, "what you just said about your book gave me an idea. Something I want to teach you. You'll like it. It's a game."

Didi was silent. She thought about her book.

"Can we play later?" she asked at last, the goodness of the morning making her brave.

"No," said her dad evenly, glancing above the woodstove. "You're going to learn now."

"Okay, Daddy."

"Go sit at the table," said her father. "I'll get what we'll need from the closet."

The closet thing was a game in a box.

"This," said her father, opening the box, "is a chessboard. The game is called chess. I'll teach you how to set it up. Then we'll go through how each figure can move and play a game, if you pick it up as quickly as I think you will."

Didi swallowed her smile again. Her dad was proud of her as long as she learned things fast.

The board looked easy like a checkerboard, but the game was like way tricky checkers. There were people for pieces instead of squat little pucks, for one thing, and all of them moved different ways. Some of the people were royal, but that didn't match how they moved. The king could only move one square at a time. It made no sense, plus you had to guard him.

The queen was exciting, though! Tall with a cape and a crown. She could move in all the directions, anywhere she wanted. Didi loved her peaceful plastic face. But her favorite pieces were the pawns, with their heads smooth as acorns as they marched uncomplicatedly forth.

"Let's try a game now," said her father after he'd gone through all of the moves. "I think you understand enough about the pieces to at least get going. I'll let you be white this one time. The player with the white pieces always goes first."

"Thank you, Daddy," said Didi, and she moved one of her pawns, glancing at her father's face to make sure she was right. She was. *Phew.* Her dad moved one of his pawns too, and then they were off, playing for real with Daddy reminding Didi about how the pieces moved when she forgot. It was hard, with that bishop moving only diagonally and that rook going back and forth. The rook looked like a piece of castle. *How can a castle piece move?* she wondered, but she zipped him across the row, singing out a happy small "Eep!"

Her dad moved his knight and grabbed her queen away. "You weren't paying attention," he said. "You've got to anticipate moves in this game. I bet you forgot how the knight even moves."

Didi nodded, cheek in her palm. "I did."

A few more moves for each of them, and it was done.

"I'm taking your king," said Daddy grinning. "I won. That's called a checkmate, and that means I won."

"You're so good at this game, Daddy," Didi said right away.

Her dad smiled and crossed his arms over his chest. Didi exhaled and smiled too. Then she went over and put her forehead against her father's. Both of them moved their heads as close to each other as they could, so it looked to Didi like Daddy only had one giant eye, right in the middle of his forehead.

DOWN

Didi and her dad were walking slap bump down the steep dirt road to the bottom of the hill. The sun was gone, long since fallen down behind the ridge, and the evergreens lining the road were blue and watchful in the dark. *Like gigantical pawns guarding a king*, Didi thought, and giggled a giggle held quiet in her mouth.

Nobody else was out walking; nobody else was on the road. Only swallows and bats and a few chickadees were out this late, darting like arrows in the trees.

Critchcrunch, critchcrunch.

Didi's dad's feet were big.

"Incompetent," he said. "They have no idea how to run a company. None."

Didi skidded and slid on the loose stones and pine needles as she hustled to keep up. It was hard work going down the hill, just as hard as climbing up, but Didi was used to it. She walked this same walk down to the bus stop every morning before kindergarten and ran back up it again when the bus dropped her off at four.

"It'd take me less than ten minutes to straighten them out."

Critchcrunch.

"Five."

"You're wicked smart, Daddy. You ought to be the in-charge guy." Didi's voice bumped and jottered in time with her stumbly feet.

Her father nodded.

Didi and her dad didn't walk down the hill every night. Only sometimes, only nights like tonight when her dad threw down his remote and reared up from his chair and said he couldn't take being inside for one more minute.

"Come on," he said. "I need a Coke."

So Didi got out from under the blanket on the couch and got dressed. Her dad stayed in the living room with her while she did, his leg jigging up and down. Then they clomped their way down the hill to get her dad his drink.

Tonight, even the air felt like a Coke, fizzing damp and cold over Didi's skin. She wished she had a jacket on, but if she'd stopped to grab it, her dad might have left without her. The house filled up with prickly not-noises when she was home by herself, now that she was almost five and five twelfths, even though her father kept calling her six. In the house alone her breath sounded raggedy and too loud, like a creature's. It wasn't fun and snuggy anymore, the way it used to be when she was little and by herself, playing chipmunk like the house was made of some stones.

The dirt road ended in a flat little bridge with the paved main street crossing it like the top of a capital *T*. Underneath the bridge, candy wrappers and clumps of foam gloamed up from the edges of a skinny brown stream.

Clatter, bump, stomp. Over the bridge they went.

After the bridge, almost beside it, Lynn's kitchen window was lit. Lynn's house was by the bus stop where Didi waited in the mornings. Lynn and her little boy Devin always came out to say hello, so Devin could pretend he was waiting for the bus too. Really he was too little. He was only three. But Lynn and Devin were inside now; Lynn's shoulder and one of her elbows were moving up and down behind the window. Doing the supper dishes, Didi guessed. She probably had made a hot supper for her and Devin, with a main dish and two things on the side like a school-bought lunch. What Didi was good at was 1) cereal, of course, and 2) soup, if her dad would reach her down the can.

Thinking about soup made Didi's stomach growl and she mooshed it with her hands.

Stop, she told it sternly. *Be quiet.*

The man at the counter of the corner store had crinkled skin and his eyes were tired and brown.

"Anything for you, little lady?" he asked when he rang up the Coke.

Her dad's eyes smallened.

"No, thank you," said Didi.

"What a polite little girl." Smile crinkles wrinkled up the man's eye corners. "Here."

He held out a piece of Bazooka gum. Didi's mouth watered.

But her dad looked at her with his mouth in a line, so she shook her head no.

"No, thank you," she said again.

"A treat for a nice little girl," insisted the man. "Please, take it."

Didi's chest squeezed in and her cheeks were hot. She shook her head no.

"Thank you anyway," she said to the man. "I don't care for gum."

"What was that all about," said her dad as they left.

"I'm sorry, Daddy."

"You don't take stuff from strangers."

"I know, Daddy."

"Then why did you even look at me to see?"

Shut up, Didi told her eyes and her poundy chest.

Her dad opened his soda. It fizzed over the top.

Ill-behaved, unregulated little girl.

Didi's dad didn't take his eyes off her as he took a good long drink of Coke.

Chicka-dee-dee-dee-dee-dee. Chicka-dee-dee-dee-dee-dee.

The chickadees saying her name helped Didi float up and get lost in their flight, their shivering, their puffing out their feathers to keep themselves warm. In the spring you could tell who was the boss of the chickadees when they came to the bird feeder.

"The head chickadee is always a male," her dad repeated now. "The strongest and most dominant. Notice things, Didi."

Slap bump down, those birds in the trees.

The alders and birches looked very climb-uppable, like ladders or stairs. So she floated—up, up, up—and held on tight to the single branch that poked up at the top of the tree.

One. She counted. *One* is this branch.

Two are the two that grow under that.

Mindclimbing down to the *three* under those. Then the counting got lovely because *five* comes next, five below three. Then

eight,
then
thirteen,
then
twenty-one,
down,
thirty-four,
down,

adding and counting and mindfloating down; Didi drifted lower, counted all the way down. No cuts, no scrapes, only soft branches blue, branches in patterns and woodflaking brown.

fifty-five, eighty-nine, one-forty-four.

Down, down, branch to branch down, boughcounting lovely till she was safe on the ground.

floated out slow from under the tree.

"—if they ran the numbers," her dad was saying, "if they

bothered to run the numbers, they'd see I have the highest per capita sales. Why are they giving me such shit?"

Didi tried taking her dad's hand.

Lynn's house again. And there was Lynn on her stoop, twisting a brightly colored cube in her hands.

Didi knew that cube. It was Lynn's grown-up toy. Each face of the cube was made up of nine little squares, all different colors: six faces of squares. It was Lynn's job to twist and twist the faces around until all of the little red squares were together on one face, blue squares on another, orange, yellow, white, green. So far Lynn hadn't been able to do it. "It's impossible," she'd said. But she liked the twisting. It helped her think.

"Hi, little bunny!"

Lynn was waving. Didi's chest clutched in.

Her dad shook his hand loose and put it on her shoulder.

"How do you know that woman?" he asked.

Heavy, heavy hand.

"She's my bus stop," Didi stumbled. "She and her little boy. She's where the bus stop is."

"Great," said her dad. "I'm sure she'll have something to say about you being out."

"Hello!" he called, making a smile for Lynn. But "I hope you don't talk her ear off, the way you go on and on," he murmured to Didi as they crossed the road. His fingers squeezed her shoulder.

"I don't, Daddy," said Didi quickly. "I don't talk."

But she did. Of course she did.

What could she do?

Help. Help. Please, please help.

"Andrew Riev."

"Lynn Li."

Don't say, don't say, don't say how I talk.

Lynn put down her cube and shook Didi's dad's hand. Two pears rested on a paper towel beside her.

"My son and I love your daughter." Lynn pushed up the sleeves of her jacket and crossed her arms, poking her fore-fingers lightly into the skin above her elbows.

Hot face, fire ears—

Didi's dad glanced down at her.

"I hope she doesn't disturb you."

Chest squeezed in, bursty and sore—

Don't say, don't say, don't say how I talk.

"Not at all," said Lynn. "She's a great kid."

head shake, no, she was not a great kid.

rumble turning. stomach churning.

tummy, rumbling loud.

"—hungry, little bunny? Can I offer you a pear?"

stone cold eyes swung down to her face

Didi shook her head no.

"No, thank you," said her dad. "We're just heading back home."

"You sure, Didi? They're super sweet today."

have to go, have to go, have to get gone

"Didi?"

Chicka-dee-dee-dee-dee-dee. Chicka-dee-dee-dee-dee-dee.

tangly up branchcount, scraping as she floated

"She just ate," said her dad.

Float, no float, no numbers helped her float with the chickadees now.

Lynn nodded, slowly, then faster, then stopped. "Oh," she said. "Okay."

She put down the pear.

Eight? Five? Three? Two?

"Where's your son?" Didi's dad asked.

Lynn looked at her dad.

"Sleeping," she said. She made a smile. "I came out for some air."

One. Zero. Zero. Zero.

"Sleepy, Didi?" Lynn asked. "You look awful tired."

Her dad chuckled and took Didi's hand in his. His fingers were tough and a little bit dirty.

Mad?

Was he mad?

Not mad?

Extra mad?

"Didi sleeps like the dead. Don't you, baby?"

Baby?

Baby? Why did he say "baby"?

Heart swelled up; she blushed and nodded.

"I sleep really good," she said, and her dad gave her hand a little shake.

"I sleep like the dead!" Didi beamed and laughed up at her dad.

The screen door banged open and Devin came out in his yellow pajamas. His face was sweaty and creasy from blankets.

"I had a bad dream!" he said and leaned against Lynn. "Hi, Didi."

No—

Lynn put her arms around Devin and squeezed him against her side. Devin pressed in close, and she hugged him some more, hugged him so tight he bent in like a circle, like the letter *C.*

"Quit staring at me," Devin ordered Didi and hid his face in Lynn's hair.

Didi's dad looked at her. His face was still.

"We should be going," he said. "Time for bed."

He let go of Didi's hand and dropped his own on her head instead.

"You better scoot up quick," said Lynn. "It's cold. Where's your jacket, Didi, honey?"

hand tightened on her head

"She's fine," said her dad. "You know how kids are about wearing a jacket."

Didi's shoulders inched up to her ears.

"I'm warm," she said. "I'm hot. I hate to wear a coat."

She looked up at her dad, but he was looking at Lynn. His smile was small and his eyes were too, his fingers pressing heavy on Didi's hair.

Lynn stood up on the stoop.

"Sleep well, Didi," she said. There was a little line between her eyes, but it mostly went away when she smiled. "We're going to bed too. It's late. Past nine." She picked Devin up and set him on her hip.

"Bye, Didi!" he said, waving. "See you at the bus!"

"Bye, Devin."

What's this; what? Lifting; her dad was lifting Didi up too, up, up, up. Over his head, onto his shoulders; what was this? What?

Lynn glanced at Didi and then at her dad.

"Nice to meet you, Andrew," she said. Then, "Take a pear with you, Didi."

She handed a pear up to Didi.

Didi shook her head no, but her fingers took the fruit.

no no no, don't take it, no no—

The pear was in her hand.

Her dad held on to her thighs.

"Say 'thank you,'" he said.

"Thank you," said Didi.

"Good night," said her dad to Devin.

His hands hitched up higher and made dents in her thighs.

"Sleep tight," he said to Lynn.

Then turning, slowly. They crossed the little bridge.

"See you tomorrow, Didi!" Lynn called as up, up, up they went, up the steep dirt road between the sleeping alder trees.

Her dad leaned forward as he took them up. The rocking and swaying made Didi's stomach churn. She held on to his head and her pear dropped to the ground. She couldn't hang on to both.

RUN

Halfway up the hill her father stopped and lifted Didi high over his head and put her down on the steep dirt road.

"Run," he said simply. "You never know when you're going to have to. Your reflexes need to be quick. And set up the game when you get to the house. I feel like playing."

"Okay, Daddy," said Didi, and took off at full speed, hoping her dad was impressed with her athleticalness as she tore up the hill to the house, even with eyes blinking from tired.

"Set the game up right," he called up behind her.

"I will," Didi heaved back, and kept running, running, running up the hill. She would set up that chessboard fast and perfect, so there would be no need for him to look at the trouble stick. Even though she hated hated hated chess.

Didi didn't want the trouble stick to ever come down. She would get untired and play her best. Her dad would win, and then he'd be happy again.

"You have something of your mother.
At first I thought not, but now
I see there is something."
                        —Nancy Mitford, _Love in a Cold Climate_

WHERE

"'Where's my mom?'" he mimicked her, voice nasal and high. "What do you care, Didi? Why should you care? Shut up right now with that whine." His hand dropped. "Don't ever ask me about her again."

You are obsessed with her

FLUKE

Zhoop . . . off went the blanket.

"Get up." Her dad was in front of the couch, the blanket and the chess box in his hand. "Get dressed. We're going."

Going where? Didi wondered as her dad moved toward the kitchen to get more coffee. She climbed into her pants and sweatshirt quick before her dad came back in the room.

The drive was long and Didi had to fight with her eyes, so they wouldn't close and make her fall asleep.

Her dad broke the quiet. "Tournament, Didi," he said. "Chess. And you need to be prepared. Get your head on straight. Quit that yawning."

A tournament. Oh no.

Didi had gone to a tournament two weeks ago with her father, and it had been very terrible, her father so angry because she didn't win, which Didi didn't understand because she did win almost all of the long games she played, but it wasn't enough for gold, her dad said. Did that mean she could have gotten him some pirate treasure if she had won?

He glanced at her now, hands still on the wheel. "I need you focused and hungry to win today."

So that's why he didn't give her time to have any Lucky Charms before they left. At least he'd be glad she was hungry this time, even though he always said her tummy rumbles irritated people.

"You came in fourth in the last tournament," her father said. "That was not good enough. I want you to win. I've entered you in the full kindergarten to grade six age group, and I expect results. Not just against other kindergarten kids. All of them."

no trouble stick

Still trouble stick marks from the last time

trouble stick marks that went "Ow" when she pressed on them. trouble stick marks because she hadn't won because she never concentrated, Didi.

Oh, please help her, God, don't make her go.

The building where this tournament was going to be was huge above Didi's head when they walked across the sidewalk to its doors. Inside were hallways and enormous rooms with big doors and curtains, lots of tables and a lot of kids—way more kids than at the last tournament and all of them with a million grown-ups with them, it seemed, and there was Didi with just her dad. There was a woman at the front of the room booming things into a microphone, so loud that the noise pounded in Didi's chest. She couldn't tell what the woman was saying or what was supposed to be happening.

"Come here," said her dad, and he took her hand to guide her through the crowd, startling Didi right out of her tiredness with his calloused palm around hers.

"Sit," said her dad, and parked her at a table. There was a boy already there, a big boy. He had five adults around him and his own chess box beside his arm. He was setting up his board, a set with ugly pieces with none that looked anything like people.

The boy must have read her mind. "We can use your set if you want," he said. "I don't care."

"Thank you," said Didi's dad, and Didi was relieved because she needed her queen with her cloak ready to float around the board, her bishops with their pointy hats.

"I don't know why we're paired up," the boy said, mostly to her dad. "She's, like, six years younger than me."

"Don't go easy on her," Didi's dad told him. "You'll have to work for it, Didi."

Didi nodded, the boy's adults standing and staring at Didi's dad.

"Play hard, honey," said a lady to the boy. She put a hand on his arm. She probably was his mother.

> *little lass by the window stood*
> *saw a rabbit running by*
> *knocking at her*

Fibonacci, Fibonacci!
Stop. CONCENTRATE.

The boy went first, fast and mashing down the button on the turn-taking timer, and then it was Didi's turn, and she was playing hard, as fast as the boy who played faster than her dad did, but it was kind of glorious to slam around the board like

41

this. Before the boy could sense her sneaking up the side, Didi got a pawn to the edge of the board.

"Exchange!" she cried and looked quick at her dad. He winked at her and nodded, and Didi turned that attention into power and looked at her choices. Lots of kids and her dad too almost always picked the knight. It was a horse that could jump over other pieces, but she wouldn't pick it, not now, not for this game. Didi exchanged her pawn for a bishop.

(even though in her head she picked that beautiful queen again and again, but not for real play, not all the time)

She had the boy's king in checkmate before he knew it.

"Hey," said the boy. "That was—amazing."

His adults all looked surprised and a little unhappy.

But Didi's dad was smiling. Then he had her by the wrist and was pulling her through the crowd again, and she was at another game with another big kid. And then another. And another and another until it felt like Didi was going to be living at this tournament place and never be allowed to stop playing chess. Didi won some of the games, but had some draws too, all against these big kids. Didi couldn't tell from her dad's face if it was okay that she didn't always straight-out win, but she knew in her stomach it wasn't.

Stay hungry

well that is no problem because I am starvingly hungry

I wish I had a burger right now

But a burger was only a rare treat and only when her dad was in a very good mood; Didi couldn't tell his mood during this tournament. His face was all blank with his hand on her wrist between turns.

There were so many voices in the room. Some kind of display on a screen at the front showed all the kids' names in some kind of order as well as the time of day. Didi hoped it was a list of people who got to go home because her name was first on it and she wanted to leave so badly. The time told her it was nine hours. Even kindergarten wasn't nine hours.

Finally it was over. No more wrist hauling. Did that mean they could finally go home? Didi's name was second on the display list, so she hoped that meant she only had to wait for one person to leave before they were allowed.

But no. Second on the list turned out to mean second place. Didi was lifted onto a little box and the loud woman gave her a cloth necklace with a big coin on it, a silver medal. Double angry, her dad was going to be, because second place wasn't winning and also guess what? She'd won most of her games by mistake. With those kids so much better and Didi getting to play with her own set the whole time. But still, too many games ended in draws. Her dad was going to be so mad, and home would be the trouble stick because she didn't win all the games.

"I wasn't sure about that first tournament, Diana," her dad said as they walked to the truck in the twilight.

He never called her by her whole name.

Angry? Extra angry or just medium angry? Please not big—

"When you came in fourth last time. Or when you beat *me* those few times. I thought they were flukes. But this seals it. Second place at states! Fantastic, Didi. Outstanding."

He wasn't angry! Even though she didn't win, he liked the silver medal and was tossing it up and catching it, over and over. Didi blushed with pleasure and stared at the shadows their bodies cast on the ground.

"Get in," her dad told her, opening the truck door. "I could have made it to Master level. Hell, my game is at Master level now. But you're going to get there and more, Didi. I give it two years until you hit Master. Three at the outside. My daughter is going to be one of the youngest Masters ever! This is the best thing that ever happened to me."

Then he went quiet as he started the car.

"Didi," he said finally. "Pay attention. First of all, we're not hiring you coaches and all that bullshit. And God knows I'm not homeschooling you so you can train for chess all day. I don't know that you even have the stamina for that kind of lifestyle. Look how slow you're still running and I've been training you with that for almost a year now."

And he turned to look at her in that way he did very rarely, upper lip raised with both sides curled, his front teeth showing.

shaky fingers and tears at the backs of her eyes

He was right. She was still slow at running, even when she ran her fastest, and she'd never be as good as he needed her

44

to be, ever; it just wasn't possible—her dad was just so much better.

Fibonacci, Fibonacci!

what was the first number were you supposed to start at

one

help God

she couldn't remember

underneath the number tumble in her head, she was wild because it would be the trouble stick when she got home

Show him your running! Run as fast you can!

But they were in the car on the highway, and she couldn't.

show him as soon as you get home! even if it's very late and the moon is there, not the sun:

2, 3, 5, 7, 11, 13, 17, 19.

Fibonacci, Fibonacci!

wasn't working and those were the prime numbers anyway and

Her dad turned his head back to face the road. What if he figured out that she had only won by mistake because of the draws, and she couldn't show him her running because they were stuck in the car again for that long drive home with no burger? He was so much smarter than she was. He'd figure it out.

Didi dropped her medal to the floor of the truck at her feet.

Mom, mommy, give me my mom.

"Help me, help me, help!" she said.

FIBONACCI

Did you know that some tree branches grow in
the Fibonacci series of numbers? One branch
at the top, then two, then three, then five,
eight, thirteen, and on and on? Adding is the
key if you want to guess the next few numbers.
You should look at an evergreen sometime, an
evergreen, evergreen, never not evergreen.

Fibonacci, Fibonacci! Fibonacci is the name
of the man who worked with these numbers
for the first time in Europe, though they were
in Indian mathematics at least a thousand years
before that.

Say "Fibonacci!" It's like saying "Abracadabra!"—
only in a sneakier way because you'll just sound
weird and smart. Like smart people in the movies
who draw math signs all over when all you truly
mean is "Abracadabra!" or "Stop!" or "Away!"

Didi, are you all right—

Didi ran toward the trees, focused and fast.

Clear. Wind. Brush. Cold. Sun like a chariot, dirt below.

Find some brush for cover, take stock, then go—
Wait.

What was that—?

A rustle of leaves like a fox in the brush.

Shut up. Listen.

Wood snapping nearby.

Again. A crackle, like a step on some twigs.

Quiet.

Then more. Then away.

Then farther away still.

Didi pivoted northwest and ran.

PART 3

DIDI: AGED EIGHT

START

Her dad was still in his bedroom so Didi ran into the bath-room to put on her T-shirt and shorts. These were her nicest ones. She tried to dress special on the first day of school if she could and these T-shirt and shorts weren't that small.

Frances Frances Frances not Schlomo—

Didi hoped she got Mrs. Frances for third grade. Mrs. Frances was bubbly and smiley and you could tell that she loved her kids.

Legs out of the pajama shorts, into the school ones.

Frances, Frances, Frances not Schlomo—

Mrs. Schlomo did not seem unkind but not especially kind either. She just seemed regular, maybe a hair on the grim side. Not the type to love her class.

The bathroom door burst open and Didi didn't have her T-shirt on yet. She covered herself as best as she could.

"I—I'm not done," she stammered.

"This isn't your house. I'll go in any room I want." Her dad rummaged in the cabinets until he came out with his vitamins. He filled a glass by the bathroom sink and put a pill in his mouth. He gulped it back like he did with a Coke all the time. But this was the first time he gulped with Didi's shirt off.

do teachers at school have locks on their doors

"Get dressed already," her father told her when he was done, so she did, facing away from him. It was hard in the cramped small bathroom. But it was all she could do.

She wedged past her father to get out of the bathroom and he let her.

DREAM

Dressed and free, Didi ran down the driveway, locust trees on either side. She shouted "Hi!" to the trees as she dashed past, even though she knew that was silly. But she was full of happiness because school and outside.

The bright yellow of the sun shone even on the wooded downhill road and Didi ran faster in its light, slipping a little on the road rocks because she was wearing flip-flops but steadier on her feet running down the hill than she'd ever been. That was good. That meant the run-up after school would be easier this year too. It always was. She remembered kindergarten when it had been so hard.

Didi ran on toward her bus stop and Lynn. She bet Devin was so excited he'd be green around the mouth because sometimes, when he was super wound up, he threw up. He was going to kindergarten at last, like a big kid, with Didi on the bus for real.

She was right. Devvie and his mother were already on their porch when Didi came to the end of her sprint. Devin was in a new shirt featuring a monster walking a smaller monster on the front. He wore new, long, slippery-looking shorts too. Beside him on the porch lay a dish of toast that Didi knew he was too worked up to eat. Her own stomach growled as she looked at it, though. She had forgotten about cereal before she ran out of the house.

don't think don't think

don't think about that

But Didi's stomach rumbled anyway.

"Happy first day of third grade!" Lynn cried. "How are you, baby? Do you want some toast?"

"No, thank you. I mean, thank you about 'happy first day,' but no thank you about the toast." She swallowed. "I'm full from breakfast at home." Her face grew warm from the lie, but at least Lynn was still talking so she had time to pull herself together.

"I knew what you meant, honey," said Lynn. "Well, we have plenty of toast because certain monster-loving boys here won't eat theirs."

"I'll barf," said Devin.

"Devvie, you've been excited for kindergarten since forever," said Didi. "Come on and eat! I'll sit with you on the bus, even. It'll be fun."

I won't be able to not talk to Devin, not after all these years of talking.

Because how else could it work? What if he told Lynn she ignored him? Lynn would know she was weird and that was worse.

There was still a bunch of time before the bus rumbled up, so Didi walked into Lynn's small side yard by the creek and shook off one of her flip-flops. She stuck her dusty foot in the water.

"That reminds me!" Lynn cried from the porch. "Didi, I had the nicest dream about you last night. We were just sitting by this creek and fishing. You and me together. It was lovely."

Didi started. "You had a dream? About me?" she said disbelievingly.

"Sure did," said Lynn. "It was really nice."

Didi laughed again and stuck her wet foot back into her flip-flop. "And we were fishing?"

"Yup," said Lynn, holding out her hands as if they were on a fishing pole. "Just fishing and watching the creek go by."

Didi laughed again. She couldn't help it. Lynn had had a *dream* about her. "Watching the creek go by," she echoed and, moving toward Lynn, laughed again.

FAVOR

"I have something for you too, Didi, before the bus comes," said Lynn. "It's to take to school in case you get bored." And she handed Didi a book. "It's all about string theory and the universe being made of membranes," she continued. "Something tells me you'll enjoy thinking about those things."

Didi blushed again. Lynn was always giving her books and Didi kept them under the couch, but still, she didn't really deserve them. She kept taking them, though, keeping them until she could read them and give them back to Lynn.

don't take it don't take it no

But Lynn took Didi's limp arm and wrapped her fingers around the book. "There," she said warmly. "Enjoy it."

Didi was quiet. What should she do? She looked at the book cover and was gripped by its image.

Then, just like all the other times, she caved in, said "Thank you," and held on tight to the book.

"Anytime," said Lynn. "There's always more where that came from. I love when you read things and give me the upshot after." This was true. Didi did like giving Lynn the highlights. It was fun to make the ideas more real with her voice.

Didi hefted the book and gripped it more firmly. A dream and a book in one morning. This was already a wonderful day.

don't think about bathroom part

Didi hugged the book to her chest.

Don't tell anyone, but Didi liked to pretend Lynn was her mother, not just Devvie's.

"Have you ever read anything by a lady called Nancy Mitford?" Didi asked Lynn now.

those books on the mantel were mom's
shhh.

"I haven't," said Lynn. "But I've heard they're arch and a little bit shocking. You're not about to read those, are you, Didi?"

"What does 'arch' mean?" asked Didi.

"Kind of playful and mischievous. Funny in a particular way."

"Oh. Thank you."

"Of course." Then: "Do you mind walking Devvie to his new kindergarten class when you get to school, honey? We've visited and played there, but I'd be grateful if you made sure he got to his room okay."

Didi felt her cheeks hollow in a way from the smile that threatened to come through, and she fixed her face so it would look like nothing to Lynn.

"The kindergarten teachers always collect up their kids on the playground before the bell rings for the rest of us to go in," Didi said finally. "I'll make sure he's with the right lady."

"Thank you, honeypie," said Lynn. "He has Mrs. Leary." Kindergarten kids always found out who they had before the first day of school. Didi wished older kids did too.

"I know her!" Didi cried. "I had her for kindergarten too. She's really nice, Devvie. You'll like having school with her."

Devin swallowed and said nothing. Then he emitted a massive burp.

Little rabbit in the wood

BUS

The bus roared to a stop. Devin had to hold on to the bus bannister to haul himself up the steps.

Didi reached out to help him but he shook her off. "I can do it myself."

They settled down in the front seat. (Devin's pick. *Nerdy*, thought Didi, but she could teach him later how to be cool.)

"I want to play race car," said Devin, all nausea having left him despite the bounce and speed of the ride. "Didi, you be my pit crew. My car is yellow, like this bus."

Play race car! Talk about not cool. But whatever. She'd promised Lynn, and it was nice on the bus. Windows open and the air rushing summer warm.

Beside her, Devvie revved his car.

Frances, Frances, Fibonacci, Fibonacci!

Stop. Pay attention to Devvie.

The bus driver glanced at Devin careering around in the front seat and narrowed his brows at him in the mirror.

"Sit still," said Didi, one eye on the driver. "That's one of the rules of the bus."

The light from the window behind Devvie made it almost too hard to see his face.

"Vroom," said Devin, and Didi imagined his race car was a chariot, taking her up, up, up and away, depositing her someplace unimaginable, someplace wonderful away in the sky.

TEACHERS

Didi had Devin confidently by the hand and walked him up across the playground to Mrs. Leary.

"Good morning, Mrs. Leary," said Didi. "This here is Devin Li."

"Hello, Devin!" said Mrs. Leary and took his hand from Didi. "I'm so excited to have you in my class." She looked up at Didi and smiled. "Didi, I still miss you. What are you reading? Thinking about anything good?"

"Not much," said Didi, but that was a lie. Here she was about to read Lynn's book and thinking about numbers all the time, but Didi knew better than to be a pest.

"Well, I hope you have a great first day of third grade, Didi." Mrs. Leary turned to the group of small kids gathered around her. "Come on, kindergartners! Do you know how to line up, so we can go inside to our classroom?"

"Bye, Devin," said Didi. "I hope you have fun!" And she walked over to the front of the school where the teachers stood ready to call out their rosters of kids.

Forget *Fibonacci.*

Didi got Mrs. Schlomo.

Blank Mrs. Schlomo who wasn't one to adore her kids.

GOOD MORNING, THIRD GRADERS, Mrs. Schlomo had written in gray on the whiteboard at the front of the room. Not even an exclamation point at the end. Didi did get to take the attendance to the office with another girl, one named Kayden, but that didn't help. She felt dirty beside Kayden's tulle-skirted self, like her hair was full of snarls, even though it was tied back with a purple ribbon she'd found wound around an alder branch at the crossroads this morning by the creek.

HOBBY

The house was small and had only one bedroom, and that belonged to her father. It made sense. He was the one who earned the money around here. It cost a lot to have a kid. And to keep up with his hobbies. Didi slept on his couch.

Last night had been hard, though, trying to get to sleep. Her father had been in an especially good mood and was walking round and round the living room. "Work's over for the week," he said as Didi lay on the couch. "I've had enough of those bozos. You must be sick of them too. Smarter than anyone in the class. What are you reading now, Didi Read-ie?"

Didi held up her book, one that Lynn had given her. It was called *Missing May*, a new skinny book that was easy to read but so sad that it made Didi's heart hurt. She was considering stopping except it was from Lynn.

"I'm going to teach you something new tomorrow," her dad said, nodding at the book. "You're going to need all your energy for this one. Put that away now and sleep."

What was the hobby? Was it another game like chess? How could she sleep all churned up with wondering? She better, though. If he was going to teach her something, she had to be alert and on her toes. Her dad was an excellent explainer, at least at first and if she got the topic quickly.

It was early and cold out, and Didi gave up sleeping. She put on her clothes and *phew* she just made it, finished snapping the last snap of the jeans she was wearing before her father burst out of his room.

"Run," he said simply, so Didi did, as fast as she could, bolting out the door to start the first of three times around the perimeter of his property, including the part in the woods. No robin-call time or watching chipmunks this morning. The hobby was bound to be a hard one and she'd better have her best reflexes front and center.

Be quick!

Be quick!

Be quick, be fast, be strong!

Didi chanted in her head in time with her running feet.

The three laps were almost up, and look there, her dad was waiting for her at the kitchen stoop, phone in hand with the stopwatch on, wearing his weekend suit, camo from head to toe.

She checked his face as she careered toward the steps. Was this going to be a good day? It was the weekend, which her dad usually liked because he didn't have to deal with work and the bozos. At home on the weekend, it was just Didi and sometimes a few of his friends who came over to play chess or cards. Weekends could be better than the weekdays, then, but only if Didi behaved. Didi tried her best. She did not act like one of the bozos and she stayed as quiet and still as she did at school. Stillness was what pleased teachers the most and if her father was in his teacher mood today, which he must be because he was going to teach her his hobby, she knew she had to shape up and look smart and do her best to be still.

"Your time's only fair to good," her dad said to her now, tapping his phone as she arrived, panting, and touched the stoop. "I want you faster. Nothing can really happen until you're fast." His voice was irritated. Not a great start.

"I'm sorry, Daddy," Didi said, but he mustn't mind her poor time as much as she thought he did. He held up a green plastic bag and said, "Come inside. I have something in here for you to use."

Didi reached out a tentative hand for it, but he pulled it back.

"Not yet," he said. "You wait for my say-so."

"Sorry, Daddy."

He nodded, once, and led her into the kitchen.

"This day is very important and special," he said. "I am going to start to teach you something that matters a lot to me and I want it to matter a lot to you as well. In a way it already does. You like to eat, right? You like when we get food?"

"Yes," said Didi immediately, and wondered wildly if the hobby was going to be Didi driving the car down to the grocery store. Oh no! How could she? She was too short and her feet wouldn't reach—

"It's an honor that I am teaching you about it today. Do you understand? I'm after a worthy opponent."

"Yes, Daddy. Thank you. I'll work hard to be a good learner."
She couldn't even see over the wheel, Didi imagined. Were his
friends going to come over and she'd have to drive them too?
Down into town or wherever else they wanted to go? Oh no—
maybe Chauffeur was going to be another one of her jobs, like
Laundry and Doing the Supper—

Didi had better be excellent and learn quick.

"All right," said her dad, and handed her the bag. "Look in
here."

Didi pulled the first thing out of the bag, a huge pair of
pants all in brown and tan and green, pants just like her dad's.
Then she pulled out a big shirt and a jacket made out of the
exact same material.

"Put them on," said her father.

Didi hesitated. Then she quickly took off her T-shirt and
put on the camo shirt. It was huge, but it was a lot warmer
than her T-shirt had been.

"Roll up the sleeves," her dad told her, so she did as best as
she could, the rolls fat as doughnuts around her wrists.

Now she had to change her pants. She'd be embarrassed if
her dad saw her underwear. But he was standing there, watching, so Didi better hurry up.

She undid the jeans as fast as she could and had one leg
in the new camo pants before the second one was even out
of her jeans. She didn't look at her dad's face, focusing
instead on the new too-big clothes. He bought them that way
to last.

She rolled up the pant legs before he had to tell her to. Then she looked up at him.

"Well?" he said.

"Thank you," Didi said immediately. "For letting me use them. I love them." It was fun to feel like a girl who got new clothes. "Could I please have something to hold up the pants, though?"

"Sure," said her dad, and gave her a length of rope from the shelf.

Didi tied it around her waist.

"Am I getting in the truck?" she asked at last into the quiet of the kitchen.

"Later," said her dad, glancing into the living room. "If you keep straight and pay attention like I ask. Don't make me get the trouble stick down."

The trouble stick was a rifle, complicated and long, positioned horizontally over the woodstove. Underneath it on the mantel were Mitford lady books, the ones that had belonged to her mom.

Please help me, God, I don't know how to drive!

"Come on," said her father, hoisting a large pack onto his back. "Get that jacket on, and grab that box by the door, then let's get outside."

"Okay, Dad," she said. The jacket hung to her knees.

What was in the box? Driving things? Tools for fixing the truck? Didi picked up the box and nearly dropped it; it was so heavy. So she hoisted it onto her back instead and tumbled out of the house behind her dad into the kitchen yard by the fence where the truck was parked. Her mouth was dry and she couldn't swallow, even though she badly needed to.

But they didn't stop at the truck.

Oh, thank you, God!

He was going to teach her background stuff first, she bet, probably how the engine worked and things like that. That would buy her time, with learning on the top of her mind while her underneath mind worked furiously to remember what she'd noticed when he was driving.

They trotted down the driveway lined with locust trees and aspens and over onto the ridge and then down. It was only when they got all the way into the valley below that Didi's mind slowed about driving. It was a little weird of a place to learn about a truck. But maybe her dad had a secret reason.

"Are we going to start with the mechanics of the truck?" Didi asked.

Her father glanced at her. "What the hell are you talking about," he said, and relief washed over Didi like sunshine.

"Squat," said her father as they reached the field's edge, and she squatted with him in the grasses cold and wet with dew even though there was the sun. "Now pay attention because this is dangerous and you don't want to get hurt."

Don't get sweaty palms. Slow down, heart.

"Check this out," said her dad and took the box from her. He prized open the cardboard top and inside was another box, wooden and quite big. Another chess set? Was he going to teach her a new play? Out here?

"Open it," her dad ordered, and Didi did. She recognized the contents of the box immediately and dropped the lid, crushing the tip of her little finger but couldn't care about that. Because inside the box was a trouble stick, broken up into pieces, lying there ready to be put together and used.

Oh, no no no no no—

What did I do, God? What did I do?

the dishes were finished and so were the floors—

also she'd read the most books in third grade—

she even went upstairs to the older kids at school for math like he wanted—

"I'm sorry, Daddy!" she cried, unable to keep alarm out of her voice.

Her dad looked over at her like she was a nut. "Now what are you talking about?"

"The . . . that . . . the trouble stick! I'm sorry if I did something wrong!" Maybe it was because she ate that can of lentil soup even though it was his favorite? But there had been nothing else left to eat in the house and she'd been so hungry, so—

"You didn't do anything wrong," said her dad, standing up with the pieces of the trouble stick in his hand. "This isn't a trouble stick like at home. This is a trouble stick for you to use, under my supervision only or you *will* get the trouble stick, and I'm going to teach you how to use it. This isn't a rifle, though. It's a shotgun. Stand up."

Calm down, heart. Dry out, sweaty hands.

Didi stood. But it was hard not to stand there and shake. "This," her father began, "is the stock. It's made of wood by a process that—"

Finally she got it. The clothes, the field, the early hour with all the birds still singing.

"Hunting?" she asked. "You're going to teach me to hunt?"

Her dad stared at her again. "What else?" he said. "You think I spent money on camo so you could look glamorous? You're damn right I'm going to teach you how to hunt. It's about time you helped provide some of our meat."

Her father hunted duck on the other side of the wood. It wasn't their property, but still. He got venison too, along the edge of the field at twilight. Deer were crepuscular creatures and that's when they liked to gather there, nibbling at crab-apple trees.

Didi's breathing slowed and her palms turned back to normal temperature. She stayed as still as she could, keeping her eyes on her father while he talked. From the edges of her vision, she saw a fox and her kits, skirting in and out of some low bushes. The kits were chasing each other while the mother fox sat neatly nearby, tail curled around her legs. Then the fox caught sight of Didi and her dad. She then barked to the kits and they all disappeared back into the shrubs.

". . . part includes the trigger mechanism. This other piece is called the barrel, and I'm going to show you how to screw the two pieces together. Take this."

Didi pulled her attention away from her peripheral vision and took the screwdriver her dad held out in his hand. Under his eye, she worked the screws on the hinge holding the stock to the barrel until she had it as tight as she could. Then her father took the screwdriver and tightened it even more.

"There," he said. "You're ready to start. We're going to start small and work your way up to bagging your own deer. Maybe even this season if you learn as fast as I want you to. Then we'll have even more meat. Here. Let's have you give it a try."

He handed her the shotgun. It was very long and hard to hold up in the proper position.

"It's not that heavy," said her dad. "But it *is* a little unwieldy, so I'm going to help you hold it at first because you're only what? Nine?"

Eight, thought Didi. *I'm eight.*

But her dad was off talking again, this time about shot and slugs and what gauges you used for what animal, and Didi was all, *Wait, what are gauges?* She hadn't paid enough attention, and what if he quizzed her? She knew he just explained it and she has *not* been a good learner, and now he was going to—

"This is how you load it," her dad was saying now. He picked up the shotgun and pushed in a slug. Then he held the stock against his shoulder. "Now we wait," he said. "A lot about hunting is patience."

Above them in the quiet, the robins and other morning birds sang. The sun moved slowly across the sky and then different birds sounded. Still Didi and her dad waited. A grackle

74

flew by, low and ready to land, and her father had shot it in its side before it even knew they were there. The bird flopped to the ground, dead. Didi was stunned from the sound of the gun. This was hunting? But that wasn't a deer. They didn't eat grackle, unless maybe he was tricking her sometimes and pretended it was a pheasant—

"Ha!" said her dad. "That's how you do it! Am I good or what? Your turn." He swung to her abruptly and then the shotgun was in her arms again. Her arms got tangled as she tried to counter its length.

He helped her hold it steady. "I won't always do this for you, though, Didi. You're going to have to work on getting less clumsy so you can hold it for yourself."

He leaned down behind her and positioned the stock against her shoulder and held her hands on the right spots on the gun.

"Look down the sight," he said. "You'll see a *V* on the post. You want what you're shooting to be in that *V*. Get ready! There's a bird! Stop messing around and shoot!"

Didi looked through the sight and saw the bird. It was a robin.

No—

"Get going!" he yelled. "Or by God I'll make you sorry!"

As if in a dream, Didi moved the barrel and kept her eye on the sight. She set the robin and the *V* together and shot.

The robin exploded into fragments in the air even as Didi exploded backward to the ground. Her dad hadn't told her that the gun stock would smash into her shoulder and hurt so bad that tears filled eyes before she could blink them back.

"Excellent!" her dad was crowing. "Outstanding! I used twenty shot for that because I wanted you to see what this gun can really do. But you're the one who sighted it! You guided the barrel perfectly! Your first time, and you got the shot!"

oh her shoulder hurt *so much*

(pieces of robin bursting and falling in a blooded rain to the ground)

God won't love me anymore.

I exploded a bird.

"So her shooting might be as good as her chess game!" Her father was grinning and slapping his thighs. Then he grew quiet. "I still expect you to improve your chess, though. I'm tired of playing these predictable rounds with you. I want a worthy opponent. Nothing else is good enough." His voice sounded like the shotgun was going to morph into a trouble stick at any moment. "Are you prepared to work harder, Didi? Are you?"

Didi nodded, tongue dry and cheeks sucking in. She had killed a bird.

—Oh, I'm so sorry, God! I knew trouble sticks were for shooting, but only duck and deer and other things that we eat

I didn't know trouble sticks were for killing robins

you don't eat a robin—

maybe God didn't see me, but I know He did

76

He'll spank me when I am dead, and He won't let me into Heaven.

"Get over here. Are you listening to me?"

But Didi was frozen. Her dad moved toward her and raised the gun.

Little rabbit in the wood—
Little lass by the window stood—

GRANDPA

Didi ran and ran. Where could she go? There was nowhere. Nowhere she was allowed where her dad might not be, and she was in so much trouble because she screamed about the trouble stick and about shooting the robin. He'd made her shoot more after that, shoot and shoot, and she did and if she listened carefully now, Didi noticed she was still screaming.

On and on she ran, in loops around her dad's property.

Wait! There were the locust trees that lined the driveway, and running along them now, Didi knew what she could do.

"Grandpa!" she called. "Grandpa!"

Grandpa had just come to live on her dad's property, in front of the house amidst the trees that lined the driveway.

"There's my girl!" And he was standing beside her, so tall that she had to look way up to see his breeze-rustling hair. "What's wrong? How are you, baby?"

I'm terrible terrible I'm a terrible girl

"Come up in my lap, sweetie," Grandpa said. "Tell me what's wrong."

The screaming stopped. Didi climbed up by his lap, although it hurt too much to sit right now.

"Tell me about your morning," Grandpa said.

No. Not that—

"Why don't we just talk?" said Grandpa instead. "Thinking about anything good?"

Didi shook her head again and touched Grandpa's hand to inspect its dry brittleness, peeling a bit but very strong. She knew roses were blossoming on the backs of her thighs, and what if they'd show below her shorts because there was no way she was wearing these camo clothes to school after all—no way, no way, no way.

"Let's look out at the view, then," said Grandpa and so they did. They were positioned perfectly to see the sun, high above the line of the mountains that lived many miles away. The late-afternoon light was the soft gold of November, spilling across the ridge.

Didi leaned against Grandpa and, finally, gingerly sat. She sat and sat. Grandpa always let her sit in his lap as long as she wanted.

"What colors do you think we'll see in the sunset today?" Grandpa asked at last.

"Red." Didi swallowed. "Then purple, then yellow," she said.

"I'm going for pink and orange," said Grandpa, his arm light against her waist.

Pink and orange. Her grandpa was probably right. Maybe because he never missed a sunset, whereas Didi sometimes did, if there were work to do or if she was inside the house lost in a book or in a thought.

"Don't you think you better hop down and get ready for supper?" Grandpa asked now.

"I don't know," Didi answered. *I don't really want to do the supper yet.* "Can't I just stay here with you?"

"Of course," said Grandpa, and she stayed and stayed.

What was that? Oh no. That voice bawling across the rocks and sticks of the front yard for her to get back in the house.

Didi jumped down and ran, not even waving goodbye to Grandpa as she went.

CHURCH

Didi liked the singing part of church but she dreaded the priest talking. He always went on for so long.

". . . a poem," the priest was saying now. "A canticle."

"'Praised be You my Lord with all Your creatures,'" he read.

"'Especially Sir Brother Sun . . .'

"'Who is the day through whom You give us light. . . .'"

In spite of the priest, Didi found herself thinking about what the poem had said about the Sun. The Sun really was a Brother, now that she thought of it. That fit to a T.

"'Praised be You, my Lord, through Sister Moon and the stars . . .'

"'In the heavens you have made them bright, precious and fair. . . .'"

Didi glanced at the paper of church announcements in the Bible rack in front of her and there was the poem the priest was talking about, right on the sheet. The part about the Sun and the Moon and more after that—Sun and Moon were only the beginning. Didi turned off her ears and read the canticle herself.

Well. That poem is super nice.

She bet Grandpa would like it.

No. Not now. Grandpa was for trees and not church. She

better pay attention again, or her father would have something to say.

Didi glanced up at her dad to see what kind of face he had and jumped. Tears were streaming down her father's cheeks and his nose was dripping, all of it unchecked.

SPEAK

"Watch," Didi commanded, swinging from the branch of one of Lynn's trees.

"Okay, honeypie," said Lynn, who was working her old-fashioned Rubik's Cube on the porch. But she stopped and tossed it gently in one hand as she watched Didi pump her body back and forth, gaining momentum, then let go in a gigantic leap. Didi landed square on her feet a little distance in front of Lynn.

"See?" Didi turned her head back to Lynn. "I've been training in between chess games."

Lynn's hand stilled and her eyes flickered from Didi's legs up to her face.

What was Lynn looking at? Were there still welts on the backs of her thighs?

No! Not anymore! Please, no more, please—

Didi whirled around, so she was facing Lynn.

That's what you get for bragging so much, brat. All it was was a jump.

"Sorry," said Didi to Lynn. Who did she think she was, still so slow at running, even though she could jog now for a very long time without getting tired. But her father wanted speed from her too. There was that to practice in the nights. Good thing she always got her homework done on the bus.

Lynn let the cube drop onto the porch. "Didi," she said carefully, "do you want me to speak—"

"NO!" jumped out of Didi's mouth before Lynn was even done talking.

Don't talk to him! Anyone! Nobody! No! He'll kill me if you tell him I talk!

Don't breathe in. Or out. Hold it right there.

Lynn's eyes looked far away. Then they pulled back to where Didi was, and Lynn shook her head. The creek bumbled behind them stream rocking over the stones.

Finally Lynn's eyes crinkled up in a smile. "Remember when Devin was a toddler and we had to pretend he was going to get on the bus to go to school with you every day too, Didi?"

"That was super cute," Didi said, and exhaled. "He would have been a very short kindergartener."

They both laughed.

Didi, are you all right—

DISCUSS

"Didi," said Mrs. Schlomo. "Come on up. Your turn." It was report card day and Mrs. Schlomo was calling the kids up individually to go over their report cards before they took them home to get them signed.

"Yours is the strongest report card in the class, Didi," said Mrs. Schlomo when Didi arrived at her desk, her face matter-of-fact as always. "Especially in math—A-plus and you go up to Mrs. Key in the fifth grade for that. She's a good fit for you."

Mrs. Key taught out of a book and Didi had already read it from cover to cover and knew what Mrs. Key was talking about, so all she did for that A-plus was keep her binder neat and get one hundred percent on all the tests. She didn't really deserve the A-plus if you considered all that.

Mrs. Schlomo cleared her throat. "Aren't you cold in those shorts, Diana Riev?" she said in a quieter voice. "There are some extra pants in the nurse's office."

Didi blushed and shook her head no.

"You're a good worker. You'd have all A-pluses if you'd join our class discussions. But I have to dock you a step for that. It's silly, Didi. Just say what you think. I know you're thinking something." Mrs. Schlomo was quiet again. "Maybe no recess if you don't participate?" she mused.

don't make me talk I'm not allowed
you can't make me talk

"Outstanding, Didi," said her dad when she gave him her report card when he got home from work. "Excellent. These are excellent grades."

excellent excellent excellent grades

if I play the game right, I'll have them in spades.

hee hee

"Thank you, Daddy," said Didi, her voice quiet, so it was almost invisible.

"Thank yourself," said her father. "You've cultivated a good reputation with those teachers and it's paying off." He broke off. "Wait a minute."

He stared at her, his face growing stiff.

excellent excellent excellent grades

remember that

excellent excellent excellent grades

"You have all As here but an A-plus in fifth-grade math. Are A-pluses possible even in the third grade?"

Lie!

Tell him A-pluses are just for the big kids!

But she couldn't. One call to Mrs. Schlomo would put him straight.

"Yes," she admitted.

"So why is it that your grades are so low in these other

subjects, then, Diana?" Her father's face was tight. "Explain yourself, please."

"It—it's . . . I can't say," Didi stammered.

"You better say."

Didi was quiet. "No, I mean I can't. . . . It's talking," she said at last.

Her father raised his hand. "You talk in that class? To other kids? Even after all the times I've warned you?"

Don't you dare talk in school. I want your mouth shut. If you talk, then it's all over.

"No, Daddy! No! I stay quiet, I promise!" Didi's shoulder curled up. "It's—it's class discussions. You get . . . docked a grade step if you don't participate. And you say not to talk, so I don't."

His face changed from anger to flat.

"You dumb little shit." Her father's voice was deadly. "The no-talking-at-school rule is for idle conversation and socializing or talking about home. Not for schoolwork. You listen to me and you listen good. You participate in those discussions and you come home the best next quarter."

"Mrs. Schlomo . . . said I was . . . the b-best this quarter," Didi stuttered.

"I say you aren't," said her father. "I expect a change next quarter and I expect all A-pluses from now on." He glanced briefly at the trouble stick. Then he looked back at her. "No excuses. Now get those filthy shorts off and go do the laundry."

He glared at her from his chair until her shorts were off. Then he got up while Didi's mind whirled.

Talk in school? How do you talk in school?

Didi was going to have to learn the way of discussions instead of using the time to think about Grandpa as she usually did now. It was wonderful, having Grandpa. Tall and gentle and kind, he was always happy to see Didi. She loved thinking about his stature. His weather-beaten skin, the soothing of sitting in his lap. A cardinal landing on his arm.

Should she show Grandpa her report card? Maybe he would be okay with it and understand about the talking.

No. Better not.

Didi found her other pair of shorts and put them on and was walking into the kitchen and then she was flying, flying through the air with the back of her butt stinging like crazy—oh God, it hurt—and then she was by the refrigerator, as still and quiet as a mouse.

"Don't you ever make me do that again for school." Her father's voice was low. "I've made my expectations clear with you since you were an infant. How dare you be less than the best possible? What's the point, otherwise? Why else am I raising you?"

Didi was silent.

My rear hurts so bad, God!

"Do the laundry," said her father. "And use the time to figure out how you're going to play this Schlomo game, talking for class. No more subpar work. I never got less than the best in school, and nothing less is expected from you."

Didi was still. He was waiting. Then she took the chance and nodded.

He held the trouble stick vertically in front of him and glared at her. Then he grabbed it up in one fist and hung it in its spot over the woodstove.

LAUNDRY

"Diana Riev!" her father yelled and Didi came running from the living room into the kitchen.

Her father was standing at the dryer, lint trap in his hand. "Is this you? Is this something you're responsible for?"

Didi crept toward him and looked in the tray. There were pebbly bits in with the lint.

Uh-oh. Laundry was Didi's job since forever. She knew better.

Her father thought so too. "You know better!" he shouted. "You've got to check the pocket of every single thing that goes in that wash. You're going to clog up this lint trap and then we'll have a house fire. Is that what you want?"

Didi shook her head no.

"Then smarten up," said her dad. "Fold this load right now and I don't want to see any paper lint stuck to the clothes. Otherwise you'll be picking it off until you go to college."

College.

College was where you went away for school when you were old. College was one of the main goals.

"I'm sorry, Daddy," said Didi. "It'll never happen again."

"It better not." Her father glanced above the woodstove, and Didi sped across the kitchen to get the laundry basket. Her father watched her take out the rest of the clothes from the dryer. A few had paper pebbles on them but not many, nothing she couldn't pick off in half an hour, especially if her father left in the truck and she could turn on the TV while she picked and folded. If there was anything left of the paper she had washed, she better find that too, before he saw it and got mad again.

Didi carried the big basket into the living room and started folding. Her underpants in this pile here, her father's in that.

Rrrrrooooommm.

The truck. He was gone.

thank you God thank you.

She folded and folded, sticking her hand into every pocket. Finally she stuck her hand in the pocket of the jeans she'd been wearing and there it was, the washed piece of paper. Didi unfolded it carefully. *Oh.* Just an announcement page from church, washed into a wad. She unfolded it. The paper was almost not like paper at all anymore, with most of its ink faded or blurred.

Wait.

This was the one with that prayer on the back, the one with the Sun and the Moon. Didi tore off the part that had the poem on it and put that piece back in her pocket. It was so soft and velvety that Didi bet it was how a chipmunk's ear must feel. It was so nice, so calming to pet.

Better be careful, though. If she touched it too often, it would disintegrate. But it was going to be okay. Despite the paper-in-the-wash mistake, Didi was generally good at keeping things straight.

WIND

"Come up on my lap, honeypie."

"I did some laundry," Didi told Grandpa. "I did it all wrong."

"I heard you had an outstanding report card," Grandpa said before she could stop him. "The best in the class."

Didi shrugged hard. "I need to do better," she said.

"You did very, very well," said Grandpa, with one, two, three birds trying to land on his hands. "Even Mrs. Schlomo said so." He paused. "Aren't you cold in just those shorts? Do you want to go get some pants from the—"

"NO," Didi said. Then she sat back in Grandpa's lap. "You want to watch me do some pull-ups?"

"I certainly do," said Grandpa. So Didi hopped down and over to the apple tree and pulled and pulled until Grandpa said, "I think that's plenty, little bunny. You are getting stronger every day."

"Thank you," said Didi, swarming back up into his lap. "Not strong enough, though. Not yet." Last night trying to move that bed frame with her father without making it wobble, she'd been terrible at that. At least it got moved where he wanted it. At least her help did that. "I have to get faster too."

The wind lifted their hair as they sat.

"I love you, Grandpa," Didi said finally and the wind wrapped around them like a hug.

"I love you too, sweet girl," Grandpa answered. Didi relaxed against him at last, even though that laundry was only folded and not yet put away and there was another load to be done.

"And if I might offer you a little advice . . . it would be to read fewer books . . . and make your house slightly more comfortable. That is what a man appreciates, in the long run."
—Nancy Mitford, Love in a Cold Climate

RANKING

Her dad turned to her without his seat belt even buckled yet and hugged her. Hugged her!

"You did it, honey!" he cried.

Honey!

"You have a national ranking!"

Didi smiled an inside smile.

"A lot of those kids in that tournament were bozos," her dad said. "Still, you beat them fair and square. And those adults you played too. The adults, Didi! That is *something*. Outstanding work. Just outstanding."

"Thank you, Dad," said Didi, her arms and back still remembering the hug.

"Your openings are what did it," said her dad, easing forward from the parking space. "I'm glad I gave you that book to study. Your openings were shit before."

Didi said nothing but she was glad she had let go and played hard in this tournament. Winning and getting points for a chess ranking mattered to her dad. Sure, hers was a terrible ranking if you compared it to some of the adults' ones, but at least it was a ranking and put Didi on the board. Maybe now the chess at home would slow down. Oh, maybe this could be the last tournament!

There were so many people in the parking lot, all of them shouting at each other and celebrating or crying, so her dad couldn't back up the car. There was even a TV crew here, to interview the famous adult players.

Didi's dad beat the steering wheel with both hands. "Come on, assholes!" he said to the cars inching past them through the lot. "Let me the fuck in."

Didi shrank back. She wished Grandpa was with her, but how could he be?

"At least now you're at my level, Didi," said her dad, nosing the car out of the parking lot at last. "At least now we can really play. I expect more consistent wins from you, Miss La-Di-Da. Cool it with the draws. You better play as if your life depends on it."

"I will," Didi promised. They followed a little green car out onto the main road.

"And don't you go bragging either, Didi," said her dad. "I don't want a new diva in the house."

"I won't."

"You'll play the guys in my chess group too." Her dad's eyes narrowed with planning. "I'll set something up. They can sign up for nights to play with you after work. Mr. Thomas. Mr. Howard. Guys like that." He stepped on the accelerator. "I'll get that started next week."

Tears pricked at the back of Didi's throat.

The ranking didn't make it over.

It was just a new kind of start.

Ahead of her, the green car disappeared off onto the highway.

TELEVISION

Maybe if she had been on TV like one of the adult players, though. Maybe if her dad had put her on camera, Didi's mother would have seen her and maybe she would have called Didi up on Dad's phone or something.

Please please *tell me.*

Where is my mom?

You are obsessed with her—

MITFORDS

Nancy Mitford is an author who wrote long
ago, back in the 1930s and '40s. She grew
up in a rich old family in England and based
her books on her own life with her gaggle of
brothers and sisters. The Mitfords had been
like celebrities, with newspapers following their
doings and parties and marriages, writing about
them with glee. In real life, though. In real life
some of those siblings had been fans of the
Nazis when they'd grown up and the Second
World War was happening. But the others had
emphatically not been. Nancy was one of the
good ones. Her sister Unity was not. Unity
stunk. She loved, truly loved, Hitler so much
that when he committed suicide at the end of
the war, she gave it a go too, with a gun to her
head. But it didn't work. She survived the shot.
Barely, though. Who could tell? Unity was nearly
vegetative. It meant that everyone else had to
carry her around and put her places and she
never said anything, not another word. Why
would someone so used to a gun make a bad

missed shot like that? It must have been some kind of mistake, the bullet dodging the most important parts of her brain, the parts that kept her alive. What a life in the end. Dependent. Silent. Bullet parts stuck in her head.

CLUES

They were hard, her mother's books, with print so small—hard even though Didi was a very good reader.

don't brag, jerk

Didi took down one of the two novels now. It was called *Love in a Cold Climate.* Well, she certainly understood those words at least. It was a cold climate right here when it was winter, cold and vast and private.

Didi tucked the book in her shirt and propped up the other one, so it stood perfectly straight on the mantel.

"What are you doing?"

Didi jumped. She'd thought her dad was outside with his bow and arrow but no. He was here behind her, watching her touch the book.

"I've told you for years that your mother's taste was shit." He shook his head. "Although those don't make me vomit as much as some of the other crap she read. But I'm sure I got more out of them than she ever did." He laughed. "Oh, Didi, those books remind me that I'm a smart man. That's why I keep them around." Then he got a Coke from the fridge and was gone.

♟ ♟ ♟ ♟

Why did he get so annoyed when Didi looked at those books? Her dad didn't mind her reading books like *The Mysterious Disappearance of Leon (I Mean Noel)* and volumes about the physics ideas she enjoyed. What was different about these?

Wait. *The Mysterious Disappearance.* Books with a puzzle. These Mitford books were special and suddenly Didi understood why. She knew! Her mother had left the books for her! On purpose! For a reason! They must be filled with clues! She left them for Didi, knowing Didi would be able to figure out the books' hints when she was old enough to read them, hints about where she was. Oh, Didi had to read them for real, right now.

"I see you're giving Nancy Mitford a go," Grandpa said as she nestled into his wood sweet lap, *Love in a Cold Climate* in her hands. "Mighty ambitious of you, honeypie. Though I heard they're arch and funny. What made you pick one up?"

Didi went quiet. She couldn't say out loud, not even to Grandpa. It sounded so stupid. But her theory made total sense.

"I'm a detective," she said at last and he nodded, a squirrel chittering on his shoulder.

"Your mother?" he asked.

"Yes."

Didi took up the book and began to read. She read and read and read.

Grandpa was wrong. The Mitford books weren't funny at all, except sometimes a little in the parts where there were kids. It was mostly about grown-ups who bolted away from everything and had affairs and World War II. A glass tub with fish swimming in its sides.

Wait. Affairs. The books had taught her what "affairs" meant and about what they were. Maybe that was the clue.

How can I find her if she bolted with a new person? Didi thought wildly. *Where in this world could she be?*

She wished her father had taught her to drive that day with the hunting after all. All around town, she'd speed, until she found the person and her mom.

"I can't!" she cried out. There were too many people in the world, even too many here in their little town. She couldn't go in all the people's houses. And what if her mother was in England or France like in the books? Didi would have to be an adult to go there. With no Dad and some money and a car that she couldn't drive and with way more clues, besides. "I have to keep reading these books!"

"Okay," said Grandpa. She tried to make his voice soothe her. "Keep reading. That'll calm you right down."

"No, it won't!" cried Didi into his branches. "What if I never figure them out?"

All alone except for her dad, Didi would be. For the rest of her life, with only a make-believe locust tree for a grandpa.

SEESAW

Mrs. Schlomo's class had earned extra recess at the end of the day because their behavior had been good. Unlike for the other kids, recess was not Didi's favorite and sometimes she hid in the corner of the classroom among the math manipulatives and read. (Never in the reading corner, even though it was more comfortable. Mrs. Schlomo could sight her more easily there and smoke her out.) If Didi had to go outside, she usually ran around the bowl of the field, training to get even faster.

"Everyone out," Mrs. Schlomo said today. "I'm locking the classroom door. We'll have dismissal from the playground. Make sure you have your planners and backpacks."

It was cold outside and Didi was too tired to run. Her dad had woken her up to do some night laps. Sometimes he did that. She still wasn't fast enough. She guessed she could take her Mitford book and reread it outside. She wished she had mittens, but no matter.

Mrs. Schlomo's third grade wasn't the only class spilling out of the school to line their backpacks up against the building and have fun. Some kindergartners were out too, playing on the equipment. Didi ran to see if Devin was there.

He was.

"Seesaw with me!" he cried, jumping down from his swing.

"Okay," said Didi. "Let me put my book down."

"How come you have your socks on your hands?" Devin asked.

"Never mind," Didi said. She took off the socks and pushed her hair away from her face and waited until Devin had taken up his spot on the low side of the seesaw. With Didi so much bigger, they couldn't really seesaw, so all she did was pump up and down with her legs on the ground to make Devin move a little lower and higher.

"Push me *up*," said Devin, bouncing, but Didi just kept them level, her eyes on the parking lot at the far end of the playground.

There was Lynn's little red car.

"I think your mom is here," Didi told Devin.

"Up and down!" Devin cried. "It's not bus time yet! My mom is too early to get me!"

Lynn saw them and waved before making her way to them across the parking lot and to the playground. Didi waved back.

"Hello!" she shouted into the cold November air.

"Hello!" Lynn shouted back.

But *BOUNCE!* was the loudest, coming from Devin. "That's what we're on this seesaw to do! Not to stay even the whole time! If you don't bounce me, I'll go and climb on the play structure."

But then Lynn was there.

"Hi, Devin!" she said. "Hi, Didi!"

"Hello," said Didi, and smiled at Lynn. Then, gently, she bent her knees and up, up, up went Devin.

"Go *faster*," said Devin. "Didi, you're not being fun!"

"Your mom is here."

"Well, honey," Lynn said. "Now that Didi's here, I want to tell her something important."

"You mean that we're moving?" said Devin.

cotton in didi's ears

little bunny oh honey
I wanted to tell you at home but here you were—

got a new job, out of state
exciting but sad—
she loved her, honeypie, she wished she could take her

Didi slowly unbent her knees.

"This is no fun, Didi!" cried Devin indignantly. "You're doing it all boring and wrong."

Lynn moved toward Didi like she was going to hug her. Didi raised her feet so fast to get off and run that her feet slid, and she went tip bang down instead. Even as Didi fell smash to the ground, Devin flew up like a bird. But Lynn caught him as he bounced off his perch.

"HEY!" Devvie roared and then burst into tears. His side of the seesaw stayed high because Didi was still fallen down on hers.

Knees tented, hands on the bar.

"Oh, Didi!" cried Lynn. "Your lip is bleeding, honey. You've bitten it through."

"I'm fine," Didi said, and stayed crouching on the board. She licked her lips and her mouth filled with a metallic taste.

"Let me get you a tissue," said Lynn, her capacious sweater billowing out all over as she searched for the pocket in its side.

"I'm fine," Didi repeated.

"Oh, honey," Lynn said helplessly. "Let me at least put pressure on the cut."

"I can do it," said Didi, letting the blood drip. "I've done it before by myself. When are you all going to leave?"

Lynn's eyes went shiny, like they were underwater. She finally found her pocket and her hand came out with a ball-point pen and a tissue. "Oh, thank God," she said and moved toward Didi's face with the tissue.

A shrilling behind Didi. School was done for the day.

The Kleenex was pressed onto the lip.

The quiet lasted forever.

Lynn pulled back the tissue. It came away red.

"Oh, sweet girl, I think you need a stitch," she said.

Didi laughed.

Lynn looked puzzled. "Come," she said. "Let me take you in to the nurse."

"No," said Didi instantly, and Lynn's face changed back to sad.

"Oh, Didi," she said. "How will I bear not always knowing how you are and if you have what you need?"

you don't know how I am now or what I need

Didi carefully pushed with her knees, so her body stood, still straddling the seesaw. She put her hand in her pocket and touched the soft worn paper in there.

Lynn was clicking the pen.

"Didi," she said, "do you have anything I can write on?"

Didi started and let go of the paper in her fingers. Her lip was tight with drying blood.

"I'll give it back," promised Lynn. "It's for you, what I want the paper for."

Didi hesitated and looked down at the plank between her knees. "Yes," she said finally. "But it's fragile. You have to be careful." And she handed Lynn her folded soft paper.

"I will," said Lynn, writing with the ballpoint on the poem side of the piece. "This is my number, Didi. For when you're old enough for a phone."

A phone. He already told her she'd never have her own phone, not on his dime, and who other's dime could it be?

"You can call me anytime. If you ever need something or just want to talk."

Didi sucked in her cheeks.

Stop, eyes. Nose, don't you run.

Crying was a sign that you were bone brittle and—

"Weak," Lynn was saying, but of course Didi already knew. "Just a week. We have to leave in seven days." Lynn was crying herself now, real tears running down her cheeks. Her voice was thick and shaky. "I should have told you at the house! Let me take you home with us now, little bunny, and you can visit a while. Run back up home when the bus would have come."

"No," said Didi. "You need a note from a parent or guardian to go with someone else out of school."

"Then we'll wait for you on the porch." Lynn hesitated. "I hate to leave you like this. I'll call the yard lady to come and help you."

The yard lady? What kind of help could she be?

"Your lip," Lynn continued, biting her own. "I really want that seen to."

"I'm fine," said Didi again, carefully so as not to make the blood crack open again. Then: "I promise I'll go to the nurse."

no I won't

Lynn was quiet, still looking at Didi.

please stop staring at me

"Okay," said Lynn at last. "See you in a little while."

no

Lynn was going. Leaving the little house at the base of the hill. Didi wouldn't bother her this afternoon if she were leaving.

I won't. Not if she's trying to leave.

Bothering Lynn. Bothering, bothering.

Had she bothered Lynn too hard? Had she talked too much and also jumped out of the trees?

I bothered her, Didi thought slowly. *I bothered Lynn the whole time.*

Her dad had been right from the start. Didi had pestered Lynn to death with her talking and now Lynn had gotten a whole other job to give herself a break.

Time passed, Didi imagined, because there were Devin and Lynn with their backs to her, almost at the parking lot.

The playground lady shrilled over the shape of Lynn's hair, calling for Didi to come to the buses. But Didi was still.

The little red car drove away out of sight.

Didi, are you all right—

Over roots and under leaves, faster, faster.

Didi's cheeks were scratched from the evergreens, blood on her face from the scrapes, but she didn't care, not now, not ever.

Thud.

Crack.

Branches being broken.

What the hell? What was that? Had she been smoked out? More than one behind her, ready with their shots?

Help me! Help me! Oh God, please exist.

Please help me. Please.

PART 4

DIDI: AGED ELEVEN

BIRTHDAY

"Happy birthday!" Grandpa called across the cold morning frost. Didi was embarrassed that she still needed him. But having some recognition of the day was cheering.

"Thank you!" she whisper-called back. She sure as hell didn't want to wake her dad.

But he was already up and in the living room.

"Good," he said. "You're awake."

She stood by the door, still wrapped in the couch blanket.

"I want you to run," her dad told her. "Three times around the perimeter of my property. If you get back before I leave for work, that can be it for the day. If you're not back, add twenty-five pull-ups with perfect form. I'll check in about that when I get home."

"Yes, Dad," said Didi. *How in the world am I supposed to prove my pull-ups had perfect form?*

Shut up, jerk. Just run fast, then. In honor of today. Get home before he's gone and make him happy.

Should she say something about the day to her father?

Selfish. You just want one of those cookies.

It was true. Sometimes, on the years he remembered her birthday, her dad brought home a cookie from the cafeteria at work. Those cookies were so good, chewy and as big as Didi's head. Didi hoped for one every year.

"Well?" said her dad. "Get dressed." Then he smiled. "After all, today is a special day, right? Last day of November?"

He did remember!

Didi beamed. "Thank you!"

"You're welcome, Didi Read-ie," he said. "What are you this year? Eleven?"

"You got it," she said.

"Great," he said. "Now tell me what you think about eleven."

"It's prime," said Didi immediately. "It's a palindrome. Also, it's odd."

Help me, what else?

Her dad laughed out loud. "I mean what goals do you have for this year? Now that you're not a little kid?"

Dumb! Quick! Think of some goals!

"I want to get stronger and faster and play Grandmaster level chess," she said finally, just as her dad's face was growing peevish.

"Excellent, Didi," her dad said and smiled again. Didi's shoulders relaxed. "Those are my goals for you too. And." He looked down at her. "In celebration of those goals, I have a fantastic present for you planned for tonight."

What? A present? Didi didn't get presents. Unless you counted the camo clothes he bought for her to wear that time when she was little. Those had been a really good buy. Didi still wore them on most winter days and they still ran pretty large. They'd last her for years if she paid attention, so she took care not to wreck them or tear the fabric where it could not be resewn.

"We're going out this evening," her dad said now. "The two of us."

"We are?" Didi laughed. Going out? Would it be to supper? Sometimes when she did well in a tournament, they stopped for a burger after. Maybe that's what he was hinting at. "Is it burgers?"

"That's for my brain to know and not yours." Her dad's eyes grew small.

dumb dumb dumb. never ask for food. just be grateful when you get it.

"Now get out there and run and earn what I got you. Otherwise it's pull-ups for you."

Didi dropped the blanket from her shoulders. She had slept in her shorts and T-shirt, and so she jammed on sneakers and ran.

Three times around. She crushed it. She knew it. Her dad was still there on the stoop.

"Excellent, Didi! That was an outstanding effort. Your best time. Ten seconds off your record."

Didi smiled internally. She couldn't help but think of the present.

Didi was so energized by the thought of the present that she ran twice around the property after school again, even though she'd run it this morning. Then she suited up in the camo clothes and waited, reading a little but mostly just waiting for her dad.

At last his truck roared up the road. Out popped her dad in his work outfit, so different from the camo he wore when he was home.

"Hi, Dad!" Didi called and he waved in answer, something round and saucerlike in his hand. *EXCELLENT!* He *had* brought her a cookie. A cookie *as well* as going out? This birthday was honestly Didi's best.

He came in. "Here you go," he said, handing her the cookie in its Saran wrapping. "Happy birthday. You're really growing up, Didi Read-ie."

"Thank you!" Didi said, and took the cookie. Could she eat a bite now? Or should she wait until he told her? *Maybe don't eat it if the present is burgers.*

"Let me change," he said. "We better have some kind of supper and get on the road."

So it wasn't burgers. Should she change what she was wearing?

Her dad read her mind. "Stay in those clothes," he said, "and today as a treat, I'll be the one to figure out supper. God Almighty, but I'm starving."

"Do you want the cookie, Dad?" said Didi immediately.

"Hunh?" he said, a smile tickling the corners of his mouth.

Didi's chest swelled.

"The cookie," she said. "Do you want it, for supper? I can just do Lucky Charms."

"You sure?" said her dad. "I brought that for you."

"I'm fine," said Didi. "But thank you. Here, have it."

For the third time he smiled. "You're a good kid, Didi." He took the cookie, unwrapped it, and ate.

The truck ride was long, but that was fine, what with the two of them going out. The night sky was clear and full of stars, air cold but every lungful wonderful.

"Where are we going?" Didi asked.

"You'll see when you see," her dad answered, eyes on the road. Then he patted her hand where it lay on the console beside him. Didi blushed in the dark. "It's going to be fun." He cleared his throat. "Should I have, ah, asked you if you, ah, wanted to bring anyone from school—"

"No!" said Didi loudly to drown out her blush. "I just want to be with you, Dad." Why would he even ask? She got along fine in class but didn't have friends because no talking outside of class discussion in school. Maybe his asking about friends was some kind of test.

"That's my girl," her dad said, and chuckled into the dark of the truck's cab. Didi leaned back.

Thank you, God.

Her dad laughed full out now and took Didi's hand in his. He bounced it lightly between them.

♟ ♟ ♟ ♟

DOODLEBUG PAINTBALL! shouted the sign as they turned into the parking lot.

Paintball? That's my present?! But that would be too much; he wouldn't want her to get expectations—

But paintball it was— "That's the surprise! Here we go!"

"Dad! Daddy! Thank you so much!" Didi had always wanted to play paintball. It sounded like so much fun, chasing people down in goggles. You shot them with paint, and when you'd got all of your opponents, you won. At least that was her sense of the game.

"We're meeting a few of the guys here," said her dad.

"Which guys?" Didi asked. "Mr. Singleterry? Mr. Cooper?"

"Yep," said her dad. "And Mr. Howard and Mr. Thomas."

"Who gets to be on whose team?"

"Well," said her dad, getting out of the cab, "I was thinking it could be us two against those four. Make it more exciting."

"Yay!" said Didi, not able to hide her smile. "Is paintball tough?" she asked as they entered the building.

"Not if you use your brain," her dad said. "Only thing you really have to remember is don't shoot anyone at point-blank range. It can hurt a person surprisingly badly and you don't want that. You just want to shoot them with your paint from a reasonable distance. It still stings, but it's not too bad."

"Got it," said Didi. "I'll be careful."

"Remember, Didi. Consider who you're playing and pay attention and think, and you'll get your opponents in no time." He smiled down at her in the evening dark. "Between the two of us, I'm thinking we won't be here too long. I kind of think we'll wipe the floor with their asses."

Inside the building, the men, all four of her dad's friends, stood waiting at the counter and, as a body, they waved.

"Happy birthday, Didi," Mr. Thomas said.

Mr. Singleterry winked.

"Okay," said her dad. "Let's suit up."

Goggles and black coveralls with old faded paint stains. Didi thought they would play outside under the stars, but here you played inside.

don't complain. he was nice enough to set up this gift. stop being so selfish.

The room they were assigned to was complicated—full of half walls, partitions, and chunky obstacles to run over or to hide behind. In a way, it was like the ruins of a city, one that had lost a war.

Phosphorescent tape showed you the walls.

"Only a quick glance at the terrain," said Didi's dad, looking down at her briefly. "I want to see how you do when the ground is unfamiliar."

"I'll do well," Didi said. "I'll concentrate. Do my best."

"Nothing less is acceptable." Her dad turned to his friends. "Lights out," he said. "Black-light game."

"To be honest with you," said Mr. Cooper, "I don't like not

being able to see in the dark." (That was Mr. Cooper all over. "To be honest with you, I hate it when the gun jams," he'd once said. *No shit,* thought Didi. *The rest of us love it.*)

Didi's dad ignored him. "Your team's green paint against our blue. Come on, Didi. Let's see what you can do."

The lights snapped out.

The men split apart and ran.

Didi ran too. What was that up ahead—a wall or an obstacle? Didi's night vision hadn't kicked in.

Stumbling. Dang! It was an obstacle after all. Didi caught herself and ran on.

Footsteps behind her. Didi's heart pounded. Could she outrun that bulk of a man? He was running like he was herding her, smoking her out from behind a partition.

Run!

She looked back and took panicky aim. A trembly

SHOOT,

and she got him. Mr. Howard.

"Ugh!" he cried, and went down, goggles shining white from the ground.

"Excellent, Didi!" her dad called from the other side of the room.

"Thank you!" she called back, even as she was running away from the sound of her own voice, so the other men wouldn't know where she was.

There. Over there. A hint of white eyeballs. Mr. Thomas. She could tell by the sway in his gait.

Her dad knew too. She could feel him come close. Didi crouched behind one of the paint-splattered half walls and carefully took aim at their opponent but

SPLAT—

Mr. Thomas overshot them, his paint landing on the opposite wall, and Didi quickly readied and took aim—

SHOOT—

Dang it. She missed him. It was Dad who spattered his friend with their glowing blue paint.

"Come on, Didi!" he whisper-yelled. She watched his goggles flash white in the dark. "You have to be faster! I want to see us win this, not go down in flames!"

"Sorry, Dad," said Didi. "I'm on it!" Her heart beat as hard as it ever had and her dad left her side for reconnaissance.

Wait, what was that?

A pause in her running. Mr. Singleterry, behind that partition?

Run? Wait? Shoot? Hide?

Footsteps upon her and a shot rang out.

Didi's shoulder.

Oh my God, it hurts so bad, oh my God, was that point-blank? Oh God! I lost for us!
She looked.

Blue paint.

Her father had shot her, not one of the men.

"TIME!" her dad shouted, dropping his gun. "Didi, I'm so sorry, honey! I thought you were Mr. Singleterry!"

"It's okay, Dad. I'm fine. Don't worry."

Oh my God, oh my God, don't rub your shoulder.

just stay still and think about something else.

Stars. Wind. Rain. Chipmunk.

"God, Didi, I'm so damned sorry. After the lecture I gave *you* about not shooting point-blank." Her dad shook his head. "Stop the game! Lights on!"

The fluorescents blared. The men gathered around.

"Jesus, Andrew."

"You all right, Didi?"

Then Dad: "Let me see your arm."

"No!" cried Didi. "I'm fine! I'm good! Please, let's just keep playing!"

I don't want this birthday to end!

Her dad hesitated. "You sure, Didi Read-ie?"

"Yes," she said, arm burning so badly that she could hardly think.

But she shouldered her blue paintball gun.

"Okay," he said. "We'll play. But be silent. Don't shoot until you see them. Watch for their teeth in the black light."

Black light made starlight, white goggles and iridescent paint from prior games on the walls.

Who was that? There? Mr. Singleterry or Mr. Cooper?

"I got him," her dad scream-whispered. "Quick, Didi! Cover my back!"

Heart pounding, Didi set herself behind her father's voice and

SHOOT!

Her dad got Mr. Singleterry in one.

"Come on, Didi! Step it up!" her dad yelled beside her. "Am I playing alone? Cooper's right there, for God's sake!"

Where? How? Where—oh! Was that Mr. Cooper shrinking behind that boulder?

SHOOT!

She got him.

"High five!" said her dad and he slapped her hand with his own. All four men on the other side down. Didi and her dad, the two of them unstoppable. Didi'd never had so much fun in her life. The focus, the fear. Her heart pounding with terror, the paint and the chase, adrenaline pouring through her with every shot.

"Well done!" her dad cried, and slapped her shoulder.

Didi cried out. She'd forgotten that blue on her coveralls. She hadn't noticed the pain while they were playing, but now it hurt much more than even before.

"Let me take a look at that shoulder, Didi," her dad said when they were back home. "God, I'm so sorry I hit you. I lost my cool when I thought you were Singleterry."

"It's okay, Dad," said Didi hoisting up the sleeve of the shirt. The welt was an ugly one, huge and raised and bruising. "It barely hurts at all. I had fun!"

"So did I," said her dad. "It was fun to play on the same side as you. We're a twosome, aren't we? A team. Quite a pair. Love you, Didi."

Didi's face grew warm. *Love you. A twosome.* This birthday was perfect. All the parts that mattered about Didi, Dad knew.

RANGE

The bus careered past the low, old, one-story homes with carports and sheds that rained along the paved road and arrived at the bottom of the dirt road hill. Didi shut her eyes.

Don't look don't look don't look at that house

"Goodbye, Didi," said the bus driver as he did every day, opening the door with a diesel puff, but Didi, as always, said nothing.

Eyes open and off the bus, running as fast as she could up the long steep hill toward home, backpack flapping heavy against her shoulder blades. Didi's stride was sure, planted, set with good push-off. She wanted to practice running without sneakers as well, though, because who knew what you had to be prepared for. Having sneakers on might not be an option. It might be bare feet. *Please not hiking boots if something happens.* Hiking boots sucked for a run.

"Come on," said her father as soon as she got in the door. "Dump that backpack. We're going out."

"Where to?" Didi asked.

"The gun range. It's time you learned to shoot skeet. I should have brought you years ago." He shook his head, irritated at the lost time. "Skeet is harder than birds."

🏆 🏆 🏆 🏆

SINGLETERRY RANGE, the sign said as they drove in.

"Is that your Mr. Singleterry?" asked Didi.

"Yes. He's giving us a deal," her dad said. "So you better shoot well."

"But I already know—"

shut up

"Shut up," said her dad. "I just said. Skeet is hard. Harder than a shotgun. It's a little puck high in the air only three or four inches wide. Your shot has to be perfectly timed. I'll give you today as a learning day," he continued as they got out of the truck. "But I expect your shooting to excel sooner rather than later. I want a worthy opponent for skeet."

Mr. Singleterry was heading toward them.

"Morning, Didi," he said and slapped her dad on the shoulder in greeting.

"Good morning," Didi said. "Thank you for letting us come." She swallowed. *Was that all right?*

"No problem," said Mr. Singleterry, so it was all right. "Are you ready to shoot?"

"Don't go easy on her," Didi's dad said. "I want her shot to be perfect."

Help me help me

Mr. Singleterry's brow furrowed.

But her dad spoke before Mr. Singleterry could say a word. "I'm here so she can *learn*. Take her out and show her what to do."

"Will do," Mr. Singleterry said.

Didi looked at her father.

"Go," he said.

So she followed Mr. Singleterry away from her father and toward the skeet shooting range. She could feel her dad's eyes on her back as she walked away.

"Here," said Mr. Singleterry when they arrived at the skeet shooter. "Put these headphones on your ears. This is loud."

Then he took up a gun, placed it in her arms, talked at her for a while as she concentrated on his words, and then finally, let the skeet fly. Mr. Singleterry was a great shot but even he missed sometimes when he was a bit too slow on the trigger. Didi's shots were wild.

CARD

"How are *you* getting mail? Who's this"—Didi's dad glanced at the envelope—"Lynn Li?"

What?

Didi's mouth fell open.

"She's the—the woman who lived in the house," she stuttered. "At the bottom of the hill."

"The one with the kid?" her dad asked and Didi nodded yes.

"I told you," he said, eyes locked on hers, ripping the envelope in half, then in half again, "never to bother that woman."

"She moved," Didi explained. Then, before she could catch it: "She was nice."

"'She was nice,'" he mimicked, flapping his hands by his face. "Forget it. Forget her. I told you not to talk!"

(it would be all over if she talked)

He raised his hand but let it fall.

Didi's mind reeled. A letter. That didn't make sense. Why would Lynn write *her*?

(Lynn had a dream about her that time, right? Maybe she'd had another dream now?)

Her father tossed the pieces of paper into the woodstove, where they flamed up and were gone.

Didi's mouth dropped. Then she swallowed.

Stop, tears, don't you dare come up—

Will she ever send me another letter?

No, idiot.

Not if Didi didn't write back. And how could she? Where would she even send a response? The address would have been on that envelope.

Besides, there would be no way to get another piece of mail. Her dad got the mail from a post office box in town and brought it home. Interception couldn't possibly be a thing.

BOOM

BOOM.

It was a few weeks later, and Didi was back at Mr. Singleterry's range. The skeet machine went off and there was skeet shooting across the sky, no more than four inches wide and so far away. Much harder to shoot than a pheasant, never mind a running deer. Didi aimed, calculated, and shot. The clay skeet shattered satisfyingly in the sky.

BOOM.

Machine went off again with another tiny skeet flying. Her dad had been right when she'd first started up with skeet. It was much more of a challenge than hunting, even for small things like ducks. It was focus and watching and timing her shot, everything else shut out. But that was what made skeet fun. The little clay puck was small but you could predict the arc of it, once you took into account the weather.

BOOM.

Didi took her shot and missed.

Ha. That's what she got for thinking she was hot stuff about knowing the weather.

TRAINING

"Go!" boomed her dad. "MOVE!"

Didi was off. The practice run he had set up would be hard, she knew. She better be fast, accurate, and ready.

Her dad was running behind her, the stopwatch going on his phone.

Didi saw the fake target duck and

BOOM—

—shot it, right in the head, fake-killing it spot on but preserving the meat. She'd get points for both.

Running. Running. At this point Didi could run for days if she had to. She'd show him her speed—

—leaping over a log and then scrambling over a boulder in her path and then along the wooded path—

There, there! A bear up ahead, the papier-mâché one that the middle school used before it changed mascots from a bear to a boar.

BOOM—

—again, right between the eyes, exploding as soon as she shot it. Today Didi was on point.

Adrenaline pumping from the bear, she ran again, the woods dense and full of roots. There was the next thing, a plywood life-sized cutout of a wolf, not to be considered meat, of course, but a predator to be taken down. Didi's steps faltered a bit as she thought about how to take the shot. The angle open to her from here was terrible, a cluster of aspens in her way. But if she moved outside of them to make it easy, she wouldn't earn as many points and her dad expected her to get the best score possible.

You have to work *to be worthy of perfection,* he always said and Didi tried but was never perfect, not nearly. Why else would she be terrified every time he woke her up for a test like this? One minute she was napping after skeet, book on her chest, and the next it was lungs pumping, heart pounding loud.

She had to go for it, never mind the trees—

Didi sighted between the aspens as best she could and

BOOM.

The wolf toppled over, breaking into shards. But she'd gotten him in the skull, not the neck, so that would be points lost. Can't keep a shattered head in the house.

Run. Run faster. Faster and faster and faster until she reached . . .

Ugh!

Her dad loved this fake creature and used it all the time, even though he knew it freaked Didi out. It was some kind of giant sculpture of a thing like a rodent and Didi didn't know which it was supposed to be. Some Australian creature, she bet, because of all the oversized rat things they had there. A wombat, maybe? No. Some kind of capybara.

Go toward what scares you. Never away.

That's what her dad always said and he was right.

"GO!" he screamed now and she took a shot and

BOOM—

—it glanced off the hardwood of the creature and went wild. Oh God, now she couldn't get all the points and he'd be even madder. She better try again—

BOOM—

Got it this time. Right on its side. The thing had a new hole but still stood, so Didi knew her dad would use it to scare her again. Her brain shuddered even as she got ready to run.

Her dad barked out another laugh and then screamed out: "MOVE ON!"

Hurtle along, run like the wind.

Her dad herded Didi through the last part of the woods, toward the fence at its edge. There was the valley just beyond it and she bet this was going to be the challenge part of the hunt.

She got to the fence and jumped over it and looked. What was next for her to find? Oh. There. A fake deer across the field, looking like a real one ready to eat apples in the twilight. Didi started to run.

Wait a minute. That wasn't a fake deer. It was real. She could see it shift as she crouch-ran toward it, trying to conceal her sound.

Her dad's excitement behind her was palpable. This was too perfect, he'd think, harder than whatever he had planted here. Didi better not blow it, not after the two shots with the gross thing—

Run.

Focus.

Sight.

BOOM.

Impact. Right in the neck.

Didi flinched.

Oh God, please forgive me—

I'm so sorry, I am—

"DIDI!"

Didi jumped. Better go get the deer and start butchering. That would give her bonus points, maybe make up for the extra shot from before.

She ran to the fallen deer, her knife ready in its sheath at her side.

"Outstanding, Didi!" her dad shouted behind her. "Excellent work!"

But Didi was already making the first cut and had her bag out to pack the meat. She didn't have this year's tag yet and it was illegal to hunt without one. But who would care? Who was going to know? The meat would be in the shed freezer in Ziplocs and he'd make her bury the rest.

RIFLES

The thing about rifles and shotguns is that you don't just shoot. You judge what you're shooting, how long, how far. Whether it's running or still. For a deer you might want to choose a twenty-gauge shot. That's enough to take one down. Unless you're asked to use an eight-gauge. Then it's a whole different story. You'll take down the deer but explode it, so you can't save the meat. Just bones, holes, fur in the air. A waste of a perfectly good shot. (Best to bury all that after, or leave it out for animals to eat. Only in the valley, though. Not anywhere else. Then there might be some questions.)

QUEEN

"Have you even had supper, sweet girl?" Grandpa said to her now, his voice quiet, uncertain of its reception.

Sweet girl. She was too old for that. But still Didi smiled interiorly a bit at the words.

"Don't worry," she said. "I'll whip up a supper right quick. Like, hey, presto, Fibonacci!"

They both laughed. Didi hadn't said that in years.

"Fibonacci, Fibonacci!" Grandpa cried too and the magic still worked. Didi leaned against the firm trunk of him and rubbed his rough skin.

"I have to finish the laundry first, though. Then I can cook."

"Oh, honey. So much you have to do. Do you want me to speak to your dad—"

"STOP!" said Didi and she leapt off Grandpa's lap branches. She stumbled but managed to surge the energy of the possible fall into a run across the lawn toward the house because . . .

roar—

—the truck was tearing up the hill.

She had to put the wet things in the dryer and another load in the washer before her dad made it all the way up the dirt road.

She switched out the loads just in time because there he was, coming through the door with a huge cubic box in his arms.

oh no. no no no, no surprise boxes, no

Her dad glanced at the washer and dryer and into the living room.

"You could at least have folded that load." He set the box down. Didi's shoulder crept up a half inch. But "Singleterry, Howard—they don't know how to play for shit" was all he said, so Didi's shoulder headed back down. "We're going to have a game, a real one, right now. I have something to show you."

He tapped the box.

"Let's open it," he said. "Didi, your knife."

Didi pulled her knife from its sheath.

Her dad had his knife out too and together they hacked at the box until it was in pieces on the floor. There before them stood a chessboard, the most beautiful one Didi had ever seen. It was a little table, with the game board as the top, inlaid wooden squares of alternating colors. And the game pieces! Each one was nestled in a space shaped just like it in a drawer below the game table, each piece carved from wood. The knight reared up on a horse, wild with battle. The bishop's miter towered high. The king was magnificent, but the one that caught Didi was the carved and caped queen, with the spiky wood detail of the crown on her head and a beautiful, beautiful face.

"You are not to touch this without my say-so," said her

143

father and Didi nodded right away. "But let's inaugurate the thing. I need a real game."

More and more chess these past few weeks. There would be another tournament. She didn't know when, though. Kept her on her toes, said her dad. You never know when you'll have to step up.

"I'm white," said her father.

No kidding
swallow that, swallow that
insubordinate thought—

"Okay," Didi said loudly.

"What are you yelling for?" But he wasn't waiting for an answer, too focused on his opening. That was good. Her dad's opening moves told Didi everything about how he was going to play, though he was better at his endgame now than when he'd been when she was small. The endgame was not Didi's favorite thing, but she studied the books he gave her and did the best that she could. Didi knew he liked to get to the end-game fast with very few pieces left on the board. Preferably just her pawn and his king. So she played and played, swiping up pawns and rooks, imagining the mitered bishops praying with the knights so they could gallop and win.

Didi protected the black queen and made her swoop around the board, scooping up whomever she could.

queen queen queen of the land
face so gentle and kind
where is our land's queen?

144

"What happened to Mom?" Didi said and clapped her palm to her mouth.

oh my God I'm so sorry

But "Why are you bringing *her* up?" was all her dad said, sounding only scornful.

"I almost forget her," said Didi and covered her mouth again.

"Well, go ahead and forget her." Her dad moved his king diagonally up one rank and over one file. "She was a piece of shit, all right? Now shut up about her and play."

ASHTRAY

Didi's face burned. How had that even come out of her mouth! Asking about her mother? He expressly forbade that!

Stupid, stupid.

Talk about stupid—Didi stared at her father's king in its new spot. Why had he moved there? It made it impossible for him to win. There was nothing she could do that wouldn't just protract the inevitable.

"Hurry *up*," said her father, so Didi did as dumb a move as she could, a knight's leap backward to reopen her ranks.

Her dad moved again, king back to his spot from his previous move.

Don't move the pawn till you have to, Didi told herself. *Better to work the queen.*

(Had her mother moved to a small cabin in the forest somewhere? Maybe she was the type that needed a lot of privacy and alone time. Like Didi. Maybe that was something she got from her mother, how about that? Maybe her mom was an author and needed the quiet to write, or maybe she was some type of scholar.

A Mitford scholar?

makes sense, lots of sense

What if I already read one of her books and don't even know it?

Because what even was her mother's name?)

Unthinking, Didi shifted her hand from the queen. She picked up the pawn and moved it two squares ahead.

Oh my God, no.

he can't win, there's no way! Oh, God!

"GODDAMMIT!" her father exploded. He picked up his heavy amber ashtray and threw it across the room, sparks exploding in flight. "Why did you have to bring up your fucking mother! Don't ever ask me about her again!"

(ashtray thrown across the room, ash raining down, crashing the ashtray and ash raining down

her mother in her cape, hand to her face

blossoms blooming on her cheek—

ashtray smashing down.)

"You know who you're like?" Her father was shouting again. "Your goddamn uncle."

What? Uncle? Didi's head snapped back, her jaw dropped like in a book. What kind of night was this? Something had ripped wide in her dad. First, talk of her mother, and now Didi had an—an *uncle*, too? Was he Didi's mom's brother?!

Her father read her mind. "*My* brother," he said. "There's nothing to wonder about him. He's dead."

Dead? Didi thought wildly. *How'd he get dead?*

"The ass died of a heart attack a few years ago. Shoveling snow, of all things." Didi's dad shook his head in disgust. "No stamina. Just like you and your slow running. And he was always complaining. 'My graduate students are taking the time

I need for my research,'" he mimicked, making his voice whiny and flapping his hands by his face. "Who cares about his damn research? Academia is just a stupid game, all about the elite. It's bullshit, that stuff. Look at me. I haven't needed a degree."

Wait, what? Her father didn't have his degree?

Too many things and Didi didn't know which one to think about first.

Did this mean he didn't want her to go to college either? Oh, then why was she bothering to skip grades and get A-pluses if she was never going to get away?

But "You're going to college, though," her father said now, and Didi sat back a fraction of an inch. "You're going to college and you're staying in. You'll be pre-law or a business or econ major. You are going to play that game and get us what we deserve."

What do we deserve? What do I deserve? Her brain was a riot of thoughts. *How will I know?*

oh God help me please

"But don't think I'm paying for it," said her dad now. "You'll figure that out for yourself."

His lip curled up on both sides, so only his top teeth showed.

Didi's heart beat fast like a drum.

run

But she couldn't.

"Go get that ashtray and my other pipe," her father said, uncurling that lip to speak. "We're playing again. And this time you play with a brain."

Saw a rabbit running by
Knocking at her door

ANYBODY

"No question," said Mr. Howard, leaning back in his chair by his chessboard. "I vote blue no matter what."

Mr. Cooper laughed and shook his head. "No matter what?" he asked incredulously and Mr. Howard sat straight up and said, "Yes."

"Both of you are morons," said Didi's dad. Mr. Thomas came in from the kitchen, his own glass in one hand and a bottle to hand to her dad in the other. During hunts, Mr. Thomas sipped gin from his canteen from start to finish, relying on Didi's steady hands for the kill. ("Gin's made from trees, Didi. So we're right in its element. I'm drinking the nectar of the woods.")

Her dad refused the beer Mr. Thomas was offering him now and grabbed a Coke instead. "Libertarian ticket all the way down is the only rational choice. Who wants the government in your business every day?"

He glanced at Didi and up she stood. "Okay," he said. "Ten minutes on each clock, men," her dad said. "Four players, Didi. One, two, three, go!"

And Didi was off, going from board to board as fast as she could, playing each of her father's friends around and around the room and all at once. It was fast and exhausting but could be exhilarating at the end on the days she played well. Rocketing round—Didi knew these men's strategies inside and out, so most of the time she'd won almost before they began.

Braggy

just because you know Mr. Howard always tries to trap your queen to one side—

don't you get cocky.

don't you mess up

But she didn't. She beat them all with time to spare.

"That's my kid!" crowed her dad, leaning back and puffing on his pipe.

"Congratulations," said Mr. Thomas.

"Good on you, Didi," said Mr. Singleterry.

"Check me out," said her father. "Look what I've done. I feel like a sculptor. I took a little girl and made a smart, strategic opponent out of her."

Didi blushed and swallowed her smile.

"Andrew, can I play her on Wednesday night?" asked Mr. Howard. "Leila is going to take the kids."

Mr. Singleterry shifted in his seat.

"Sure," said her dad magnanimously. "Any of you, take her when you want. I'm opening up the schedule. And I'm adding something new to the package too. Hunting. The kid's already bagged two deer this year alone, as well as some duck and a turkey. Bow and arrow with those. You can take her out with you, and she'll get your meat in one shot."

don't promise one shot

perfect shots are harder than chess

A couple of the men started, but Didi knew they wouldn't speak up about it being illegal for her to have shot two deer. Not when her dad was making such a kind offer.

The (baby's) wails now entered on a crescendo, and the whole room was filled with hideous noise.

"Poor soul," said Linda. "I think it must have caught sight of itself in a glass. Do take it away . . ."

—Nancy Mitford, *The Pursuit of Love*

DOLLAR

Gym. Today was basketball. Red and blue pinnies. Seventh-grade gym was good. All you had to do was show up, be respectful and play excellently. In fact, it was good not to talk in gym because being quiet counted as respectful. The kids that clustered in twos and threes and fives on the court in their pinnies before the game started didn't care about that, though, and their chatter made a din in the gym.

"We get Didi," one of the boys was screaming. "After the drill, for the game."

"Kyle, you're captain. You pick her."

"Okay," said Kyle. "I'm on it."

There were too many kids for the drill, so Mr. Doppler cut the class in half. Didi was in the first group, red pinnies against blue, taking turns taking shots at the same time. Whoever sank the ball got a point for their team. The drill was rapid, with Didi *dribble, dribble* running fast and sinking her shots.

"Yeah, Didi!"

Didi was silent.

"Well, whatever, that was a hell of a shot."

thank you

Her group was finished; hot and sweaty from the drill, Didi sat with her back against a freezer at the end of the gym. The gym doubled as the school lunchroom, and this freezer was where the lunch people kept the Popsicles you could buy for a dollar after you ate. Didi had never had one because how was she going to get a dollar? Her lunch card wasn't loaded for that. The Popsicles looked so good, though, even though they were made out of real juice and not the bright colored fake kind, because school always made the lunch healthy. Still. Right now, so hot. Just this once it would taste so delicious.

Kyle was in the second group, racing up now against Vincent, dribbling and ready for his shot. Vincent threw his ball before Kyle, from the three-point line. Kyle was on his toes, though, and zoomed his own ball across the court and knocked Vincent's ball right out of the air. Someone quick passed him another ball and he took it to perform a layup to the basket.

"Yes!"

"He, like, shot the ball out of the air with a *ball*!"

"He's the shit!"

"In all the ways," and off some of the ones who liked boys went with their shrieking.

Home.

"Dad?" Didi asked. "Can I . . . have a dollar?"

"What the hell for?" Lips already tight.

"They sell Popsicles at school," Didi stumbled, despite the warning. "Healthy ones. I thought it could cool me down. After playing hard in gym."

"Are you sinking your shots?" he asked sharply.

"Yes," said Didi, nodding her head.

"Where do you think this dollar would come from?"

"I was thinking." Didi swallowed. "Maybe one from the men money."

Her father raised an eyebrow.

"From when I go with them hunting," Didi stumbled. "Or play chess."

"That's not your money to use," said her dad, his mouth now a line. "You didn't earn it."

Didi could feel her forehead making a question mark before she could help it. Hunting alone the whole time with men, to whom there was nothing to say and who had little to say to her. Tramping around the woods for eternity just this past weekend with Mr. Howard behind her, eyes on her body as she walked. And she always had to report the get when she got back to the house. Had to get the meat in one.

"Who does all the schedule management and schleps you to wherever they want to hunt?" asked her dad. "Me. Wait until you *really* have to work. You'll know what earning means then." He stared at her and shook his head. "'Popsicle,'" he mimicked, and Didi's cheeks burned with shame.

It was late and the house was cold. Didi wanted to get the blanket and go to sleep, but her dad was still on the couch watching TV. But then he stood up, tall and full of purpose. Didi flinched.

What had she done now?

But "I'm out for the night" is all her father said, putting on his coat. "I'll be back when I am."

"Okay," said Didi.

"I want you studying this, though." Her father handed her a book from the end table. It was called *My System* with an old-timey man on the cover. Clearly about chess. At least the cover promised 419 diagrams.

"Don't rest on your laurels while I'm gone, Didi. You may have clinched that tournament last week, but there wasn't much competition there. Read that book and learn something. I expect to see a change in your middle game."

Middle game. When would her dad stop going on about her middle game?

"And here's the pistol, just in case," he said, punching the code into the electronic lock on the gun case. "Keep it under the pillow. I don't want anyone prowling around my property."

"Okay," Didi said, and put the pistol under the pillow that went with the couch.

The wind picked up, and predictably, the house creaked. Didi knew that it was just weather and walls, but those noises freaked her out a bit when she was alone. Anything could come up the hill to the house, right? Or up from the valley and over the ridge?

Never mind. She had the pistol under the throw pillow and she could sleep in sneakers too.

be ready, Didi—

Maybe reading the chess book would help.

The book was long, and Didi was exhausted. She just had to stop. At least she was alone to change into the T-shirt and shorts that she slept in. She lay down on the couch under the blanket. The pistol was hard beneath the pillow under her head, so different in every way from the frayed paper she palmed in her hand.

What was that?

Didi swung her legs over the edge of the couch and stood up, listening.

It's nothing, she told herself. *Just that window in my dad's room. It always rattles in wind. Come on. You're being as dumb as a character in a horror movie.*

Horror was her dad's favorite.

Didi sat back down on the edge of the couch, elbow on her knee and her palm under her chin, fingers against her cheek. She let the palm creep up to cover her mouth. Who would care if she wasn't here? Nobody, that's who. Her dad would be happy, because except for the money she earned—

not earned—

—she was nothing but a burden. And her mother gone, too. Like the woman in the Mitford book who hated her own baby—her mom must have seen Didi's face in a glass.

Was there something wrong with Didi's face? Hard to tell except in the bathroom at school and Didi was rarely in there. There were no mirrors here in her father's house. She knew her hair was messy all the time, though, because all she had to comb it with was her father's tiny barber comb, and it pulled too hard for Didi to bear using it every day. Her purple ribbon kept it back, but that was as good as she got.

(*I'm too okay to help—too good at school, never any trouble*
All that overrode her messy hair.)
it doesn't matter.
She had Grandpa and outside and the soft paper in her pocket and that was more than enough.

Face in her palm, Didi sat until the wind died down and there was the moon. Then she touched the pistol under the throw pillow and put her sneakered feet under the covers and finally fell asleep.

SURPRISE

"Hey, presto, Fibonacci!" Grandpa called to her through the dawn. "There appeareth my granddaughter! Come sit," he said as she drew closer. "I have a surprise to show you. And something to say."

What? Didi perked up. Was it something he'd figured out about her mom? Grandpa still felt the Mitford books held something, some clue, and that they should keep rereading them to see, though Didi was long past thinking that was true.

"Good morning," she said and coughed. There was a virus going around at school and it wasn't very bright of her to come out in the winter dawn in just a T-shirt and shorts.

"I don't like the sound of that cough, honeypie," Grandpa said sternly. "Hop on up."

Didi hesitated and coughed again. "Aren't I too big for sitting in laps?"

"Of course not," said Grandpa.

"I don't want to be some weirdo that still needs to sit in a lap."

"You're not a weirdo."

Right, Didi thought.

"Or you're a weirdo of the best stripe. Come on, sweet girl. There's something beautiful you need to see."

So Didi climbed up into his lap and relaxed a little against his chest.

"Close your eyes," said Grandpa.

Didi touched the paper in her pocket and blinked.

"Don't worry," said Grandpa, knowing her mind. "I'll keep watch for your dad. I have to show you the morning!"

"I've already, like, seen the morning," said Didi.

"Well, you're going to see it in a different way," said Grandpa firmly. "Eyes closed. It's safe, Didi, honeypie. He's still gone, not home."

Finally Didi closed her eyes.

"Head to the right," Grandpa said and she felt his twiggy fingers on her cheek as she turned. "Good. Wait. Now open! Don't stare directly. Look off to the side."

Stare directly at what? There was nothing there but the sun, creeping up over the opposite ridge. It was almost fully risen and Didi already knew better than to stare at the sun.

But Grandpa was speaking:

"Praised be . . . all . . . creatures,
"especially Sir Brother Sun,
"Who is the day through whom You give us
 light. . . ."

Didi started and sat straight up.

"The canticle!" she cried, turning to look up at Grandpa's face as the last of the wind blew through his leaves. She coughed. Then: "I've read it like a million times!"

"Outstanding," said Grandpa. "Very special. That's why I wanted you to think about the Sun. And now that you've seen your Brother, my girl, close your eyes and turn your head left."

Obediently, Didi closed her eyes.

"Now open," he commanded, and Didi did. To her left hung the fat moon in the sky.

"Fibonacci, Fibonacci!" Grandpa cried. "What's that for a piece of magic? Sun and Moon out at the same time!" And he was reciting again:

"Praised be . . . Sister Moon and the stars,
"In the heavens you have made them bright,
  precious and fair."

"You have to admit there's magic at work here, Didi. Fibonacci, Fibonacci!"

"What's magic?" Didi asked. The Sun being out with the Moon? That happened every once in a while anyway; it wasn't all that rare. But it was true Didi hadn't seen it like this before, the Moon nearly plump as a plum and not just a slim crescent as the Sun rose up beside her.

"Yes, indeed, Didi the Moon. Magic."

"Why are you calling me the Moon?"

"It stands to reason," Grandpa said. "If the Sun is your Brother, who else would you be but his Sister, the Moon? I Fibonacci'ed them into being out there together for you this morning. Yourself and your sibling, by word of a saint."

Didi smiled. "Fibonacci, Fibonacci!" she said, and this time it was a toast to Grandpa. "It *is* beautiful," she said. "Thank you. And thank you for the canticle. I know all the rest by heart."

"I know you do," said Grandpa. "Want to say it now?"

And Didi found that she did.

MANSLAUGHTER

The truck reared up the driveway. Her dad was already home? He didn't even bother to go into the house, just jumped out of his truck and into the shed at the top of the driveway. He came out awkwardly, a plywood board in the shape of a person in his arms. Oh God. He was going to practice shooting. Something must have pissed him off so that he needed to shoot in order to blow off steam. Didi was glad it was the plywood person that'd get the steam and not her, though it creeped her out whenever he shot at that. Too close to the shape of a real person. It even wore a hat.

What should I do? Stay put here? He couldn't see her up in Grandpa's lap, not if he were going to shoot toward the ridge. Or should she just jump down, run across the stump-filled lawn and get to the house? That's where he'd assume she was.

"Assholes! Fucking bozo assholes!"

He was already setting up now, placing the person and its stand on the ridge. He paced backward from the target with his gun drawn, closer and closer to the locust trees but not taking his eyes off the target to look beside him. Didi sat frozen in Grandpa's lap, Grandpa himself wooden and still behind her.

"FUCK your demotion!"

SHOT! SHOT! SHOT! SHOT!

Her father was good, with both a pistol and a shotgun. Not dead center good though. He was so right-handed, his shot fell just on the edge or to the side of the plywood person's heart every time. He never had Didi shoot at the cutout, but it happened when they shot together with the bull's-eye too. It frustrated him no end. Didi had some ideas about how he could fix it, but she knew better than to speak up about that.

And obviously right now she wasn't going to say anything at all. A demotion. Oh, sweet God, the bozos at work had won.

Don't let him see me, don't let him see

(Why doesn't he compensate his shot for the right-ness?

how dare you even think that how dare you)

Didi's chest started to tickle, a cough on the rise.

No, she told herself. *No coughing until he's done.*

Watch other kinds of trees: the aspens and some firs. Now. She meant it.

But she coughed.

"GET DOWN HERE!" he shouted. "NOW!" Had she ever seen him so angry?

Didi got down and ran, Grandpa calling her name behind her.

"Hiding up in the locust trees? Your special place to what, spy on me?" Her dad was furious. "Fine! Come on! You want to see shooting so bad, shoot yourself! Move the target! Now! Set it up by your little hiding place!"

Didi's brain was breaking but he had the gun and was so angry so she picked up the person and carried him over to the locust trees and then went back for his stand.

"Never mind with the stand!" said her father, setting the plywood shape against Grandpa. "We'll just prop this on your little hidey-hole and see what you can do."

He shoved the gun into her hand.

"Focus!" he said. "Get him in the heart in one. No more bullets than that. You better be perfect, or I'll have your hide for a rug."

No—

What?

The plywood man in front of Grandpa—

Oh Grandpa help me please!

"Just pretend it's like paintball, but shoot it in the chest," Grandpa called. "It's fake—you're not hitting a real person."

but it felt like it, it felt like it, she couldn't go for the heart

wasn't this like practicing manslaughter?

Didi had known that word since she was five and read it and thought it meant a man's laughter, evil, like "mwa ha ha," but now manslaughter lay in front of her, and a man's laughter rang behind her as her father watched the gun shake.

Now no more laughing

"Shoot!" screamed her dad.

I'll go for the upper arm

like paintball like paintball

She raised the gun and sighted.

"No!" her father yelled. "Move that gun over! Aim *properly*! I told you to go for the chest!"

terror tears at the backs of her eyes

"You don't want the chest?!" shouted her father. "Great! Then go for the head. Blow his brains out, Didi! Come on, now, Diana! SHOOT!"

he grabbed her arm the gun went off, went wild, oh my God look where it

struck—

Grandpa right in the chest

his skin splintered in flight

Didi shot, she shot her own grandpa

oh grandpa not grandpa oh grandpa I'm sorry! but it was too late because she already knew he was dead.

Manslaughter. Didi fell forward onto her knees.

Too much—he was dead. She'd killed her own grandpa, shot him right in the chest. She couldn't get up, not even to go ascertain the wounds. She knew what there would be to feel.

Shot, sprayed in his bark. Splinters of wood. A blown-out lap of branches.

She could never make the tree be Grandpa again.

first Lynn and now Grandpa, and it was her own fault again. Worse this time, infinitely worse—

Didi bent over her knees and sobbed and coughed and sobbed some more, her dad still screaming behind her.

INFINITE

Rat-*tat-tat-tat*. Rat-*tat-tat-tat*. Rat-*tat-tat-tat*. Rat—

Shane was practicing to be a drummer, cracking at the top of his desk with the edge of a ruler. He sat right behind Didi, his desk sticking out beyond the end of the row. If he weren't there, Didi would be in the exact corner of a perfect square of English Language Arts students. Last Tuesday, Shane had stolen an X-Acto knife from the art room, and now when he wasn't drumming, he took sheet after sheet of paper from the bin on Mrs. McMennehy's desk and sliced it all up, slicing and slicing whenever Mrs. McMennehy had her back to the class, slicing and muttering and slicing some more until he had a pile of jagged paper ribbons on the floor at his feet. He hadn't used the X-Acto yet today, but Didi kept listening for the *zsst zsst zsst* of its blade.

Rat-*tat-tat-tat*. Rat-*tat-tat-tat*. Rat-*tat-tat-tat*. Rat-*tat-tat-tat*—

Mrs. McMennehy was in her usual spot up at the front of the room, writing something on the whiteboard. The windows were open. There was no sun and Didi was cold. Tired too. She didn't sleep much last night.

—*manslaughter*—
don't be so stupid, it was just one of the trees
manslaughter
But there were crusty things in her eye corners, even so.

Click. The minute hand of the clock snapped from 7:59 to 8:00. Didi took up her pencil and drew a skinny-thin line from the left side of her desk all the way across to the right. She put a tiny "0" where the line ran off her desk at the left and a tiny "1" where it ran off at the end on the right.

Rat-*tat-tat-tat.* Rat-*tat-tat-tat.* Rat-*tat-tat-tat.* Rat-*tat-tat-tat*—

"Today we will continue work on our new ELA unit." Mrs. McMennehy tapped the word she'd written on the whiteboard.

MEMOIR, it said.

The minute hand snapped over again: *click.* Class periods were each forty-one minutes long, and there were eight of them, not counting lunch. One minute of ELA had gone by. Didi rubbed her eyes and looked at the length of the line on her desk. At its halfway point, she drew a vertical hatch mark across it, about six inches long.

One down, forty to go.

"Who'll help me by passing out the homework journals?" Mrs. McMennehy asked.

Rat-*tat-tat-tat.* Rat-*tat-tat-tat.* Rat-*tatta-tat-tatta-tat-tatta-tat*—

"Kyle, be a good human and help me, please," Mrs. McMennehy said.

Kyle got up to be a good human and moved up and down the rows, the weight of the homework journals stretching his arms out into a skinny triangle.

"I really enjoyed reading your entries last night, kids. It was fun to look at the photographs you chose. You were all such adorable babies."

Liar. Didi bet Shane was a troll baby.

"*Tikka-tikka-tikka-tikka-tikka-tikka-tikka-tikka*—" Shane's tight, fierce lip whispers shot over his rhythm and across his desk and into Didi's spine. Her shoulder blades hunched toward each other, and the clock clicked over another minute.

Didi eyed the distance between her line's vertical midmark and the "0" on the left edge of her desk and made another mark halfway between those, a little bit shorter, maybe five and a half inches long. Minute number two at the half of the half. Two minutes gone, thirty-nine to go.

"Of course there were a couple of you who did not complete the assignment and I'll see you at lunchtime to make that up."

"Bite me," Shane hissed.

rat-*a-tat*-rat-*a-tat*-rat-*a-tat*-rat-*a-tat*-rat-*a-tat*—

Bite me bite me bite me bite me

Click. The third minute ticked over, but Didi was distracted as one of the girls dropped a triangular wad of paper onto the floor between her desk and one of her friends'. The first girl had super nice hair, long and brown and curly. The other one had on new clothes. Her leggings were ankle length, and Didi's pants were too, though not on purpose like the leggings.

Pay attention, she told herself. The third minute mark went halfway between the "0" and the mark at the half of the half, landing an eighth of the way over from the start of the line. She made this mark even shorter, maybe five inches long.

The leggings girl leaned down to pick up the note. She

read it and laughed over at her friend. They saw Didi watching and stopped, widening their eyes at each other.

"Pow! Pow! Pow! Pow!"

Rat*atat*rat*atat*rat*atat*rat*atat*rat*atat*rat*atat*rat*atat*rat*atat*rat-*atat*rat*atat*—

"Are those leggings new?" A whisper. "How'd you get your mom to let you have a pair with so many rips?"

For a minute, Didi thought it was Mrs. McMennehy who was asking about the leggings but then that didn't make sense.

"She took me to the mall last night," the leggings girl whispered back to the hair one. "To spend the gift card I got for my birthday. I hid these with the nerd ones she made me try on and switched them on our way out of the store. I changed into them this morning in the girls' room."

They laughed. The laughs sounded like little screams.

Kyle moved from kid to kid, the weight of the notebooks making him rock like a baboon. Didi had to pee, but she better stay put. She'd already missed some directions.

Click. Fourth minute. Fourth mark, halfway between the "0" and the last mark she'd made: half of the half of the half of the half. This hatch mark was four inches long.

Half of the half of the half of the half. Half of the half of the half of the half.

"Kids." Mrs. McMennehy looked over at their part of the square, and the girls quieted.

Shane did not.

Rat*atat*rat*atat*rat*atat*rat*atat*rat*atat*—

"I'm so looking forward to getting to know each of you better through your writing in this unit," Mrs. McMennehy continued, shifting her gaze.

Didi's head itched and she put it down on her desk. The desk was sticky and smelled like erasers and paper towels from the girls' room. From down there, her line looked enormous, stretching from her nose to the edge of her desk near the wall. The ghost of yesterday's lines were there too, gray and faint and almost exactly underneath the one she was making now. Her hair fell over her elbow and her fingers bumped against the cowlick on the top of her head. It was sticky too, stiff with grease.

Plop. Kyle dropped Didi's notebook on her desk. There was a yellow Post-it sticking out of it, right by her eye.

"Please take a moment to look at my comments, everyone. Head *up*, Didi."

Head up, head up.

Behind her, Shane cracked his ruler faster. His mouth noises were rigid and piston-thin.

Rat-*tatta-tat-tatta-tat-tatta-tatta-tatta-tat-tatta-tat-tatta-tat-tatta-tatta-tatta—*

"Pow-*zsst-zsst*-pow-*zsst-zsst*-pow—"

zsst-zsst-pow *zsst-zsst*-pow *zsst-zsst*-pow

right into Didi's spine, spine scrunch stomach roll and loud

pew pew pew

(shards of a bullet, someone shot down)

1, 2, 3 1, 2, 3 half of the half of the half of the half 1, 2, 3 1, 2, 3 grandpa lynn devin three half of the half of the half of

Didi's head swerved one way and her stomach the other.

(shards of a bullet, someone shot down)

I want to get out; is it time to get out?

She started to put her pencil away, but her smallening midpoint lines reminded her. Not enough of them yet for the period to be over and it was only the first line of the day. Seven to cut before busses and home, then back here tomorrow for a new set of lines, and the next day, the next day, the next after that till the end of the year, then the year after that, after that, after that—

"Open your notebooks, Didi and Shane!" *RAT!*

"Die, bitch," Shane hissed.

diebitchdiebitchdiebitch

Didi opened her notebook. *Didi,* said the Post-it, *Where is your picture? If you are not comfortable letting me see a baby photo, choose a more recent one.*

A more recent one. Didi laughed, and the class turned to stare at her.

I hate this I hate this I hate this I hate

(shards of a bullet, someone shot down)

Rattarattarattarattarattarattarattarattarattarat-tarattarattarattaratta—

1, 2, 3, 1, 2, 3 grandpa lynn devin three 1, 2, 3, 1, 2, 3 grandpa lynn devin three

"—pretty if she brushed it—"

"—tried to play with her back in first grade?"

all the words were muffled as if cottoned

Didi didn't remember putting her head back down on the desk, but it was nice to be there, even so, surface smooth under her cheek. But she was behind now, in marking the halfway points. She had to catch up.

midpoint and mark, midpoint and mark, midpoint and midpoint and midpoint and mark.

The marks were getting closer to zero, exponentially closer, geometrically closer, and closer and closer to each other as well, tighter and closer and shorter each time, but when she looked from the "0," it looked like they were growing, like volume increasing like a scream getting louder.

(shot scattering, somebody down!)

"—always wears that little girl shirt—"

stop stop stop stop

When they were in first grade the other kids used to play chase

Didi's face was in flames

RAT RAT RAT RAT—

The kids were all standing now and moving all over and Didi didn't know why or what she should do. Why were they moving and what were they doing? Didi hot and sweating and stuck in her seat.

Did I make did I make the mark for this minute I don't know don't remember don't remember I don't—

RAT RAT RAT RAT!

174

don't care, what's the point, there are so many days filled with too many lines and too many marks

RAT! RAT! RAT! RAT!

there's never an end to the halves I make either; you can always take half and a half of that too

RAT! RAT! RAT! RAT!

the halves just get smaller but never quite get there—I get close to the zero but never can land

pencil   drop   arms   stuck

"—partners—all—topic for sharing—"

up on the whiteboard there was written in red

MY EARLIEST MEMORY

(*—you are obsessed with her. what about me? I'm the one you married*—jesus christ, she's three and can read. she multiplies too. you're pissed off because she's just like me—*you are obsessed with her!*

car   blue   slam   gone)

didi was floating and gone and away from X-Actos

"Please partner with Shane, Didi. Share before writing."

away with her halves getting smaller and smaller

away from the car and her mom and her grandpa

"Please partner with Shane, Didi. Share before writing."

Straight as an arrow, Didi was running, flying, sun high overhead. Almost through the valley. Sneakers cold and damp.

How could she use the valley in her favor? Stay out of its center, that's for sure, head around to the side where it faced on the slope.

No! That was stupid! Was it stupid—?

You dumb, unhinged little shit. You better know where to run.

Brain jumbled and full of adrenaline, Didi ran on, up and up the valley. Faster. Faster. Go!

PART 5

DIDI: AGED FIFTEEN

CLUB

Chess club. Prep for October Insanity, the intermural school version of basketball's March Madness, teams playing teams from other schools in a whirl of competition, brackets and winning and advancing forward with a lot of cheering and snacks.

"You join that team," her father had said unexpectedly when she got to high school. "Those matches and your games with me and the men are something, but this will keep your game up as well. I've seen the guy who runs it at the adult chess nights in town. He's pretty damn good."

A Super Ball flew across the room toward Didi now. Mr. Nomura, the coach, had given Super Balls to the whole team after a big win last year and it was a rare meeting of the club that saw them not fly.

Reflexively, Didi threw her own ball up to hit the ball out of the air, but she missed and it bounced off Aiden's desk and onto his head instead.

"Ow!"

"Point!"

"Calm down," said Mr. Nomura over the cackles. "Focus, people. Eyes on the demonstration board. I've set up a play. What would be the next best move for the white side?"

Didi glanced at the chessboard projected onto the Smart-board as the other members of the chess club settled in and fished snacks out of their backpacks.

That game board. Didi shook her head. *Best move is to quit the game. That play's not going to go anywhere.*

"Anyone?" he asked now. "Didi? Thoughts?"

Didi hated this kind of attention. All eyes on her in jeans ripped but not in the cool way and this camo shirt so old and so small.

Finally, Didi spoke: "Give up." She shrugged. "Stalemate. No one can win."

"Exactly!" said Nomura and the room applauded.

Didi shrunk inside her shirt.

"Tell us why, Didi."

Please leave me alone.

But she spoke. "Pawn's protecting black king. Knight on white." Didi swallowed. "No one will be able to move."

Please let me stop now.

But no. "Come up and show us," said Mr. Nomura from the Smartboard. Didi shook her head no. All that talking already. She just wanted to get to a game.

NO

The end of October Insanity. Didi was already in the chess club room when the rest of her teammates came in, roaring and wild with backpacks and insults.

"You're a dumbass!"

"You're an assface!"

"SHUT UP! WE ROCK!"

It was Halloween and the team had won their final match against Edmonds High yesterday afternoon, which meant they were going to November's state competition.

"You are a total Philly cheese steak," Dallin said to Aiden now, fists bashing lightly at his friend.

"The hell I am, you smothered pork chop," Aiden replied.

"What the hell are you two talking about?" asked Lexie.

"Shut up, pepper remoulade. This is between men."

"You gender-conforming shit," said Lexie. She was new to the chess club, ninth grade, the only other girl besides Didi. "Women are who run this team. Right, Didi?"

Didi, leaning against a window, didn't answer. Outside, the wind blew through the school's athletic field, making the grass at its edges swing and sway. Most of the kids, Didi included, would stay inside here in the warmth of Nomura's room until five or six tonight. Mr. Nomura never cared. When he wasn't helping with their chess, he was grading or preparing his classes for the next day. "A win-win," he called it, and Didi thought it was nice of him to say it like that.

"Way to go yesterday!" Nomura hollered behind her, over the din. "Now that was some chess you played!"

"We smashed them!"

"Yeah, we did!"

"We killed!"

"Let's face it," said Lexie. "Didi's the one who won it for us."

"*All* of you were great—some of the best playing I've seen from you," said Nomura. "Though you are right that Didi's playing was exceptional."

The wind was stronger now, bending the branches of the trees that lined the field.

Nomura paused.

Then: "Okay, kids. Match yourselves up by level and get out your boards. I'll come around in a minute. And we'll talk again as a group a bit later." He cleared his throat. "I have some stuff to tell you."

Dallin moved through the desk clusters with the team's box full of treats, into which he had just dumped a bag of fun-sized candy bars. "Take what you want, sweetie," he said to each of them as he passed by and the kids took fistfuls, chewing as they paired up for games.

Not ready to settle down, Didi didn't bother to pair up. She left the window and wandered around the room instead, glancing down at the games. Lexie and Pascal's board. She shook her head at Pascal.

"Why, Didi? Why can't I win this?"

Didi swallowed and pointed to Lexie's phalanx of pieces.

"No way to get through. No breakthrough," she said. And she drifted away from the table.

"HA!" Lexie crowed. "I KNEW I could beat you, Pascal! You and your Lexie-Is-But-a-Child."

The racket of the players continued, Didi still meandering round.

"Mr. Nomura, my opponent took a piece that wasn't there." Dallin was plaintive, but Nomura paid no mind.

"What the hell are you even talking about," said Oscar.

"K to C6," said someone at another desk cluster.

"Ack! I don't know where to move."

"Just use your rook pawn."

"Why? That's a shit ending."

Just simplify the calculation. Square the pawn. Contain the king.

Didi better quit playing everybody else's games in her head and play her own before Nomura noticed. She played against herself almost every meeting of the club, black and white together, unless Mr. Nomura played opposite her. Didi hated when he did that because kids always crowded round to watch when that happened and even the thought was enough to make Didi's shoulders hunch.

She picked up a white pawn and moved. Countered with black. *Focus,* she said to herself. *Play.*

So she did, on and on until Pascal interrupted.

"Didi!" he yelled from across the room. "All I have left is double pawns. How can I win against a king-queen combo?"

Think three moves ahead. Maybe five. Maybe eight. See where she's going to go.

But Didi was quiet, focusing once more on her own game.

"—should have defended your own queen, weirdo—" Aiden was disgusted with Dallin now.

"I might have to triangulate."

"Maybe. No, yeah, I see what you're doing."

In Didi's game, both sides had already lost their queens. She thought for a moment and picked up a bishop. But before she could make black's move, Mr. Nomura spoke.

"Listen up!" he said. "Sorry to interrupt. But I think we better talk now."

Hands stilled all around the room.

"Did any of you hear about last night's board meeting?" Nomura asked.

"Ew, no. Snorefest."

"I didn't even know there was one."

"There was," Nomura said. "After your match against Edmonds."

"What about it?" asked Aiden. "What happened?"

Mr. Nomura shifted at his desk. "They didn't approve the bus for us to go to the state competition, or the money for the hotel."

"What?"

"Come on!"

"This is *states*!"

"What was their reasoning?" Mark asked.

Mr. Nomura shrugged. "Football made states too. All the extracurricular monies got funneled to them. They didn't expect we would win." He sighed. "I did what I could, kids, but no."

The room erupted. Aiden's king burst through the air. Didi grabbed a bishop and hit the king as it flew through the room before it could land on its target. Which was just the whiteboard, but still.

"It's always effing football around here!"

"Why don't they care we made states too?"

"They never care about any of our wins!" Oscar stormed. "Why would they care about this one?"

"Okay, you all, from now on we quit spending our money on all this candy and put it in a kitty instead—"

"Yes! And start baking for bake sales. Every day this week."

Mr. Nomura just shook his head and sighed. "Fundraising is a great idea," he said, "but honestly, it would take a whole lot of bake sales to get us to states, and we only have three weeks."

Dallin's jaw dropped. "What the actual fuck," he said.

Didi glanced around the room at the others. Sure, it sucked, but there'd be other games. It's not like they were going to win and make nationals. Brynnwood, who'd play them at the state competition, was a bigger, richer district. They paid for masters and coaches to come in and teach their kids. Didi's school had Nomura and Didi.

"Thanks for fighting for us, Mr. Nomura," said Pascal.

"Of course," said Nomura. "Why wouldn't I? You and this club matter. Remember that. Please, go back to your play. I'll be up here in case anyone wants to talk more."

The room was quiet.

"Ugh," said Lexie at last. But she picked up a rook, and because Nomura asked them to, the other kids started up again too. Outside the window, the wind strengthened considerably, pushing against soccer goals and straining against the field's loose wire fence.

Didi turned back to her board, but what was this? Mr. Nomura, sidling his way through the desks toward her.

Oh no. He's going to want to play me.

But it wasn't that at all. "Didi," he said quietly, leaning over his hands on her desk, "can we talk about your homework?"

Homework? Not a game? Nothing about states? But when he wasn't opening his room at lunch and after school for the chess club, Nomura taught Western Civilization to the eleventh grade. Didi'd already read the textbook at the start of the year, a thick mess about groups of people swarming like ants over other groups, and then more groups swarming over those and conquering them. Again and again. Ruined walls, old mosaics, from way back to right now. It was depressing to see it all written out like that. The homework had been to start a draft of a paper about prehistoric warfare, and Didi, knowing the whole book was going to be more of the same, had been too weary late last night to bear it.

"Are you all right, Didi?" asked Mr. Nomura. "It's not like you to not do your homework. What's going on? Were you too tired after Edmonds?" He hesitated. "The past couple weeks, you've seemed . . . exhausted. Is there something— Do you need me to speak to—"

"No, I DON'T!" Didi's hand knocked a plastic queen to the floor. Outside, the wind blew harder. *Calm down.* "Please. I'll make it up, Mr. No—"

She was cut off by a knock at the door.

"Come in!" yelled the team.

"—mura," said Didi. *please don't call my dad*

The principal, Mrs. Reed, leaned in from the hallway, her hand still on the doorknob.

"Oh," said Pascal. "Hello, Mrs. Reed."

"Hello, Pascal. I'm glad to see you contained for once. Mr. Nomura, can you step into the hall for a moment?"

"Sure," said Nomura. "You all keep playing." And then, quietly, back to Didi: "I'll check in with you again later." And he moved out the door with Mrs. Reed.

The door shut. The chess team was quiet.

"Maybe they're talking about states."

"Shut up," hissed someone. "Pascal, can you hear?"

"Only as well as you can," said Pascal from his seat by the door.

It was true the murmurs from out in the hall were impossible to discern.

Then the murmurs grew louder into words they could all hear:

"I did the best that I could—" Mrs. Reed.

"You voted to fund their damn football!"

Whoa.

"Go, Nomura," Lexie said quietly.

The talking outside grew even louder. Didi bent to pick up her queen. Her hand shook as she made the next play, sliding the black bishop diagonally over near the white king.

What if he's fired? Will I have to go back to regular tournaments and home right after school and just playing the men and my dad?

oh God please no

No one else was still working their board but Didi. White rook sliding over to protect its king, a black pawn advancing to meet them.

Mrs. Reed. "—don't know who you're speaking to like that, but you're certainly not speaking to *me* like that—"

Now Nomura's voice, forcibly: "What are we running here, Joanne? A school or a health club?"

Silence from the hall.

"Yes!" cried Aiden, pumping his fist. Some other kids hooted out too.

Shut up! Stop! Bishop takes the black pawn!

But it was clear Mrs. Reed had heard them. "That's it!" she shouted. "Jeff, you're done. Insubordination. To myself *and* to the board."

She murmured something else, too quiet to hear. Then nothing but footsteps and silence, except for the wind.

Finally Mr. Nomura came back in, red-cheeked but steely eyed too.

"Nomura!"

"Are you in trouble?!"

"Don't worry!"

"We got you!"

"You're good kids." Mr. Nomura wiped a hand across his forehead. "I don't know what all is happening."

"Will they let you keep coaching us?"

"I don't know," said Nomura.

what will I do if they make him give up the chess club—
oh my God where will I go?

Didi grabbed up her backpack without putting away her board and got the hell out of the room.

WARNING

Didi pounded against the wind up the dirt road hill toward the house. Sweaty. Cold. Behind her the mail van roared past along the road but no little-girl hope now about it turning up the hill.

Home. Didi slammed inside the kitchen to throw her damp camo shirt into the washing machine.

Arms over her head—

Her father burst in, the rifle in his hands.

"Goddammit, Didi!"

"I'm. I'm. Getting—"

oh God why is he home—

grabbing her shirt back out of the machine.

"Why are you so late? Where were you?"

"School," sputtered Didi, arms down now and crossed over her chest, camo material covering her. "Chess club ran late." Focus on the particle board walls.

Her father's eyes were ice. "Get your shirt on," he said and Didi put the damp shirt back on as fast as she could, her arms confused in the sleeves.

"Who'd you play?" he asked before she was done.

"Me," said Didi. "I played myself."

"How'd you do?"

"Stalemate." Didi almost couldn't get words out. "I lost both queens."

"Fuck!" he exploded and Didi was flying, flying across the room, momentum from his swing smashing into the back of her thighs. Didi caught the woodstove on her hip. She bashed into the mantel and managed to get her hands up fast enough to save her face but still crashed down onto the floor. The Mitford books fell down around her, covers open, spines bent.

"Excellence, Didi!"

Iron-hot pain traveling through her hip and spine.

"Excellence every time! Or else why have you play in that club?"

Her dad placed the rifle back over the woodstove.

"I'm so sick of you," he said.

Body hurt so bad—

Stay still. Don't think.

Crouching on the floor.

"You and those fucking assholes at work. Those idiots! It's obvious that demand algorithms fuel sales! But they're all about the cult of personality over there. All about who's an *extrovert!*" Her dad whined the word, closing his eyes.

Unbidden, Didi's hand reached across the floor toward the Mitfords.

"Fuck them!" Her dad's eyes were open again, glaring and angry.

Didi's hand froze.

"Those fuckheads fired me."

"Wha—?" Didi started, and stared up at her dad.

"SHUT UP!" Her dad bent over her and Didi toppled back off her haunches. "Why, you think I want to work for people who can't see the bigger mathematical picture? I could fucking double their yearly profit margin!"

What? He got himself *fired* this time? What were they going to do?

(What an ass.

No wonder my mother had to leave)

Shut up! Shut up! Don't you start with that, don't wear that thought on your face—

"Oh," her father said, his lip lifting in his snarl. "So you think you're better than me, is that it? You think you wouldn't have been let go?"

Love in a Cold Climate. The Pursuit of Love. Still splayed open on the floor.

Her father tracked her gaze. "Those fucking books!" he shouted. "They suck! The first five pages of one was all I could stand. Why are they so important?" He laughed a hollow laugh. "Why is anything? Seriously, who cares? It's all over now anyway! I can't wait ten years until you're through with college and grad school for you to show those bozos out there what's what! So what the fuck is the point of raising you?" His voice was high. "But obviously those books are more important to you than anything I'm saying, aren't they, Didi?" Whining, hands flapping: "'My mother was so wonderful!' You think she was so amazing, Didi? You think she was so great?"

Her dad leaned down and grabbed the books up in his hand. Before she could help it: "No—!"

"'No—!'" he mimicked her, and slammed open one of the books. His eyes swept across the words. Then he stopped and snorted, finger stabbing at a page. "See? Right there. One of the best ideas I ever had. I got more out of these stupid first pages than your mother ever could have gotten out of the whole book."

What was he talking about?

Her dad looked down at Didi and barked a laugh.

"Why don't I just study them for a minute more, Didi? Then maybe I'd be as all-fucking-perfect as you! Right?"

Didi dropped her head.

"That's it, isn't it? You think you're the shit!"

The pain was a duller blade now. *Stay tight. Stay small. Don't get up until he tells you.*

Her father held her in his stare. Then he raked his eyes down another page, and another, and another, Didi motionless on the floor.

He looked up, eyes unseeing. Then he grinned. Then laughed again.

"Oh my God," he said. "Oh my God, this is perfect. Now they've given me another idea. Who cares what the hell I do?" He threw the books back down on the mantel, covers and flyleaves akimbo. "You know what, Didi?" he said. "You're right. Those books are great. Perfect. You are too. Fifteen and you're perfect. You're exactly what I need you to be."

He turned to her, grin gone, eyes made of steel. "Be grateful," he said. "Consider that fair warning. It's time. See how smart you are now."

And he turned on his heel and was gone.

WHAT

Didi stood. The backs of her legs were on fire, her body rigid and taut.

Grateful? Grateful for what? Grateful for—

(trees, the valley, the sun overhead?!

grateful, I'm grateful, I'm grateful, I'm great

shut up shut up shut up shut up!

no work, oh, god, he'll be—)

Shut up, Didi! Stop it. "A warning," he said.

Warning? A warning? What warning? What?

Calm. Think. What did he say? Mitford books. How shit they were. No warning in that.

But more—the pages. The first few gave him an idea? But he only ever said her mother's taste was crap!

(you've got that right.

shut up shut up

don't you think like that don't)

Something with the reading, though. One idea formed some time before and another just now? Was the warning contained in that?

Look! Check! The books lay on the mantel where they'd been slapped down. Which one had he been reading from?

Didi didn't know. She had to read the beginnings of both. Now.

Wind howling behind her, Didi's fingers were frantic, tearing at the cracked glue and bent spine of the first book.

Oh, what was she even looking for?

Love in a Cold Climate:

"*This book is dedicated, by gracious permission, to Her Royal Highness, The Grand Duchess Peter of Prussia . . .*"

No! Nothing here. Nothing that sounded a warning. Hurry, read the next book!

The Pursuit of Love:

"*. . . on goes life; the minutes, the days, the years, the decades, taking them further and further from happiness . . .*"

No, no, no, no!

Look for more clues! Start The Pursuit of Love *from the beginning!*

First page.

"*Over the chimney-piece . . . hangs an entrenching tool, with which, in 1915, Uncle Matthew had whacked to death eight Germans. . . . It is still covered with blood and hairs, an object of fascination to us as children. . . .*"

Didi stood still.

Oh my God.

The entrenching tool over the fireplace. The rifle, the trouble stick he had made to serve in its place, hanging heavy over the woodstove.

This was the book, then. These were the pages he'd read. This was the first idea he had gotten—the trouble stick! Why had she never noticed it or made a connection before? She was so stupid!

Eyes fixed on the window, the locust trees in the driveway. Last of their leaves all fallen from the windstorm, mitered branches towering high.

Come on! Hurry up! The other idea—she had to find it! *Turn the page—again, again, again!*

Words jumped out.

"'If wishes were horses, beggars would ride. Child hunt tomorrow, Janny.'"

Didi almost dropped the book. She did, but her reflexes even in this moment were strong. Fast. She caught it before it hit the floor.

The second idea.

Didi read it again and she knew.

The child hunt. A child hunt. Hunting a child.

Not a deer, not a bear.

Not playing Fox Run in the fields for fun, as in the books.

Work. Ballistic.

Her dad wanted to shoot.

She was no use to him now.

"So what the fuck is the point of raising you?"

He was going to hunt down a child.

A child.

His own.

With a gun.

"'Help me, help me, help!' she said.
"'Ere the huntsman shoots me dead.'
"'Come, little rabbit, come with me —'"

Her mom sang softly,
with Didi in her lap.

SKEET

BOOM.
SHOT.
skeet scattered from the sky, so cold out here, but Didi
didn't care
BOOM.
SHOT.
hadn't missed a shot yet

reload and
BOOM.
SHOT.
skeet scattered from the sky, Didi's heart pounding like
someone was coming for her, her body terrified but her mind
straining to be clear and steady, separate from this hammering heart and sweaty forehead.
BOOM!
SHOT!
here. now.

reload.

again.

missed. shit.

But even so, it was better this way, knowing it was coming.

She just didn't know when. Tomorrows kept coming with nothing in them, but Didi knew it was on the way.

WHEN

Oh God! Help me! When?
   (don't you talk or it'll be all over)

when when when when when when when when

CRACK

Kids. Chess club. Picket signs for states: SAVE OUR—

BOOM.

SHOT.

skeet scattered from the sky

Backpack at Didi's feet resting against the legs on one of the desks on which she—*what?* on which she—

BOOM.

SHOT.

she hadn't missed a shot yet

Pascal was rapping. "WE'RE THE FUCKING BEST! BETTER THAN THE REST! YOU OTHER MOTHERFUCKERS CAN'T FUCKING CONTEST!"

Aiden juggled chess pieces in the corner. King, bishop, pawn.

"WE'RE THE FUCKING BEST!"

"Shut up."

Oscar was diagonal to Pascal.

"I agree we are the fucking best, but you rapping right now is not exactly helping us get these signs painted—"

(You are obsessed with—)

"Classic? You want something classic? How about this, then?"

Pascal began to sing, a scratching in Didi's skull:

204

"'By the LIGHT of the silvery MOON—'" until—
reload and
BOOM.
SHOT.
—a bishop bolted into Pascal's neck.

"WTF, dude? I mean, talk about classic! That's great-grandpa music! Classic Doris Day!"

Oscar's king on Pascal's face. His mouth dropped open, but it was already—

"'. . . of the silvery MOON . . . !'"

"Shut up!" Lexie was fierce.

"All right, you all," Mr. Nomura said, swinging through the door. "Let's get some chessboards out."

"Mr. Nomura!"

"You're still allowed to coach us?"

"I think so," he said. "The union is totally behind me. Come on. Let's get going. Look up here at the demo board."

"But Mr. Nomura—"

"We're making protest signs—"

"What else can we do to help?"

Nomura shook his head.

"Nothing," he said. "We just have to wait. Other heads are at work on the problem." Gestured again to the demo board. "Eyes up here. Let's take a look—"

the board. a setup of one of Didi's from last week

stomach shrunk

right now he wanted her to demo?

Not with that talking of yours—

BOOM!

Didi jumped a mile. Other heads looked up over their posters.

"Just a book," said Mr. Nomura, glancing from his desk to the floor.

SHOT.

skeet scattered from the sky, Didi's heart pounding like someone was coming for her, her body terrified but her mind straining to be clear and steady, separate from this hammering heart and sweaty forehead

Mr. . . . Mr. . . .

Nomura

leaned down to pick the book up.

"It's called *Grandmaster Secrets: Endgames.* It's a good one. You all should read it. Speaking of endgames, let's look at this beautiful play."

"Whose was it?" said Pascal.

Aiden said, "You know it was Didi's," and everybody did know it was hers.

"Come on up, Didi," Nomura urged her. "Tell us about how you developed your moves from here."

But Didi stared down at the chessboard before her.

"Come up," Mr. Nomura said. "Head up. Please."

"Didi!" cried Aiden.

Her head snapped up.

"Did you know that tree branches often grow in the Fibonacci series?" she said. "One branch at the top, then two, then three, then five, eight, thirteen, and on and on? You should look at an evergreen sometime, an evergreen, evergreen, never not evergreen."

There. *Now just leave me*

little rabbit in the wood

The room was quiet now at least.

leave her what

Thank God because all that noise of these teenagers teenager-ing around.

alone.

At the front of the room, Nomura hesitated and then cleared his throat. "Let me show you all what I saw on Didi's board—"

"Nomura!"

BOOM!
SHOT!

Bishop flying through the air.

King hurled out of Didi's hand so fast, she hadn't even thought. But she missed the bishop. There it was on Aiden's chest instead.

Didi's heart beat so hard, she thought it might burst all over the chessboard, perfectly laid out but for the queen.

Fix her.

Didi centered the queen on her square.

What if Nomura is fired too—

She wasn't armed the way it was her human right to be.

—oh God please help me but He never really did

reload.

again.

BOOM.

SHOT.

missed.

The overdrumming in her heart would not still.

PREPARED

No sleep, not for days, though she faked it when he slept.

Stay up. Be ready.

Outside the window. Sun, pale yellow and low with the dawn. November light streaming, the air frozen and cold.

What was that?

I can't see what's down in that valley—

(*stay ready, be ready, stay steady, be rea—*)

Four men. Camo. Swarming up over the ridge. Canteens strapped to their belts. They were here. She should have known it would be something with them. So many days since his warning. She'd waited. And now came these four men.

be ready be ready get ready get rea—

"Stand up."

Didi jumped, arms wild.

"Get dressed. I want you prepared." He looked at her, smile playing around his lips. "You know what this is. I practically told you. It's time to see what you can do."

TIME

Men crowding into the kitchen, everyone in camo, including
Didi.

thank God I'm all the way dressed

thank God

oh God, help me,

please, help

A big bag lay at Didi's dad's feet.

That shape, were those gun lumps in that bag, shotguns
ready to go—?

"Here," said her dad now, dumping the contents of the bag
out onto the floor. "I got these."

What?

What were those?

Her father stooped to the floor and Didi could barely make
out the paintball gun in his hand.

Didi went limp as a noodle and sat down.

*That's it, that's all, that's all we are doing? He's hunting me with
paintball, is that all it ever was? Oh, thank you, God, thank you, I
thought it was real—*

"Didi's and my guns are different colors than yours," her
dad told the men. "Didi, the game is that you have to get all
the men before I do. All four of them should have your color

on them before mine, and none of them should get their color on you. That's how you'll know if you won." He looked at her. "Play hard. I want a worthy opponent. A game between equals. You get your paint on these men, or I win."

And he glanced above the woodstove.

Didi was so weak with relief, she couldn't stand up.

"What are the parameters?" Mr. Thomas asked.

"Yeah," said Mr. Thomas. "How far out can we go?"

"The boundaries of my property. You know them from hunting with Didi."

The men nodded.

"Okay," said her dad. "Hide well. Get her. Your team is yellow." Then, to Didi: "You have the rest of the morning to shoot them."

He stopped.

"You don't want me to beat you."

And he glanced above the woodstove again.

Mr. Singleterry looked at Didi and then at her dad.

Didi's dad might beat her. He might. Four of them and she had to get her color on them all first.

"Go," her dad told the men. "You've got half an hour's head start."

The men crowded back out of the tiny kitchen and started to jog across the lawn, scattering in all directions.

"Don't watch them," her father said and Didi snapped her eyes to his.

"What color am I?" she asked, looking at the two paintball guns on the floor.

"Red," he said and gave her one of the paintball guns. The other lay waiting on its side.

"What color are you?"

Her father laughed.

"Orange," he said. "Though I guess"—and now he leaned right over the woodstove—"you could say I'm also red."

And he took the rifle down from its place.

"I get a head start on you too," said her dad, voice low and even. "Ten minutes. The last ten minutes of this half hour we're giving the men. Then it's on." He looked at her. "Don't you dare let me beat you."

Didi shook. "At—at paintball?" she asked, and he laughed and laughed.

"You dumb little shit."

beat her, he'd beat her, how could he not win?

her with a paintball gun and him with a rifle—

"Play tight, play right, hunt them down and don't let me get to those men first. I don't want to find you if your paint's not on those men. I want to be proud of you, Didi. Listen. Look at me, Didi. I'm not kidding."

Didi nodded, perched tight on the side of the couch.

"Stand the hell up," he said and she did.

"I'm not through with you yet," he continued. "You get those men, Didi. Or it'll be all over. I'll finish you, Didi. You'll be gone."

Didi's mouth dropped and she shook.

Right, right, I was right the first time

He'll finish me, I'm going to be gone

"Come on, Didi," said her dad. "You know you're perfect for this. You're the ideal, perfect prey."

He held his rifle steady, barrel tipping toward her.

Gunman there, gunman gone, gunman there again. Didi's pounding heart would not still. The practice, the running, all the chess and the shooting. A worthy opponent. That was everything he'd ever wanted her to be.

VIGILANT

Didi didn't know how the minutes passed as her father held her in his gaze, but twenty must have gone by because he stood up now and said, "I'm going. Again, there are ten full minutes before the men's half hour is up, and I get the full ten for a head start on you. Ten minutes before you can leave to find us all. I'll set the chess timer and go. Ready?"

Pound.

Click.

Her father took the rifle and paintball gun then was gone.

Click.

Click.

Click.

Click.

Eternity in the seconds.

Plan, make a plan, what kind of plan could she make? What kind of plan would even work?

Proud of her? Rid of her? Rid of her—

Gone.

at least then maybe there's rest

START

Bzzzzzz.

Her dad's ten-minute head start was up, and so was the half hour for the men.

Didi bolted out into the yard, paintball gun in her hand and canteen strapped to the tactical belt wrapped around her waist, chipmunks chattering behind her.

oh God, help me God, please exist, help me

I don't want to—

not right now, not right here, today—

Where to run? They could be anywhere, behind or in front of her—how could she pick a direction and go?

Quick. Think. Who would her father try to find first? She'd have to be fast to get there before him with his massive head start.

How can I know?!

But Didi's feet were already running northwest toward the field, sprinting away from the house.

Clear the board is his way. Easiest pieces off first. Until it's just one piece against his last—

GO!

Her running. Her training. Her body was a machine.

Crouch low! Quiet! Anyone could hear!

215

Didi hunched down and moved forward through the grasses in the tamped-down path to the field and paused when she reached its edge.

Stop. Listen. What can you use?

Silence. Birds. Chickadees and robins. No rustles, no movement, nothing she could see. What was she thinking, running to the field first? Would anyone ever hide in such an open space? Maybe she hadn't been thinking, just running so fast—

Stop!

Near the woods. A beech, grown stout with pear-shaped leaves. A dark shape shifting behind it. Which man was it?

OFFENSE

The answer came to her as soon as her thought.

Mr. Cooper.

The easiest.

Her instincts had been correct.

All those nights her dad made her play him—Mr. Cooper often left his offense wide open, like he didn't even realize defense was a thing.

The shape shifted and started to run. Mr. Cooper, his heavy body running. Turning sideways to sight her.

His shot went wild but not Didi's—

SHOT.

Hit. She got Mr. Cooper in one.

Oh please no orange on him, no orange, please none

She ran to look at laughing Mr. Cooper.

Paint all over it. But just red paint, no other.

thank you—

"You got me!" Mr. Cooper yelled and fake fell to the ground.

Shut up! He'll know where I am! He'll find the other men first and I'm dead!

Didi sprinted away and along the edge of the clearing toward the woods.

ASPENS

Running. Running. Feet flying through the frost-melted field, Didi was aiming her body straight into the woods. This was where the rest of them would be, right? Best hiding places were in the trees.

Stay off the deer trails and keep to the brush. Make it harder to be seen, if not heard. Branches from firs clawed at her face, but Didi scarcely noticed. Still more conifers ahead and all around, evergreens as far as the eye could see.

evergreens, evergreens, ever the evergreens

(*Three laps around the property, then can I stop?*)

Ahead. The cluster of aspens.

Go around! Those trees are too thin—

SHOT

rang above her head

Didi immediately dropped to the ground.

Was she hit? No. No paint on her clothes. But there was yellow paint on the aspen in front of her.

Who? Who was in here? Where were they hiding?

The wind rustled in the stand, everything quiet but for gold-turned leaves.

Focus. Think! Didi crouched up silently and moved forward along the line of the trees.

There. A man, squatting down, stealthy. Trying to stay hidden while he prepared for his next shot. He glanced up and he and Didi locked eyes.

Paintball guns lifting and ready to shoot—

But Didi was first, and she shot Mr. Thomas red, almost without thinking.

She should have known it was him all along. White in his camo and he liked those slim trees. He said deer never even knew you were there.

"Got me, Didi!"

"Did I get you before my dad?" Didi huffed as she ran away from the red on his shirt.

"Yes!" Mr. Thomas cried. "Go! Run! This is fantastic, am I right?"

Didi ran.

THINK

Think! Didi remonstrated with herself. *Plan. Don't be an idiot. What would Mr. Singleterry do? Mr. Howard?*

Mr. Singleterry was the best shot, the best at moving through the terrain. He'd be much farther away by now. Hardest to get—and that's who her dad would save for last. So Mr. Howard, then. What about him? His big chess play was to try to isolate her queen to one side of the board. To one side of this stand and the property was west. Would he be trying to squeeze her there?

Didi swerved in that direction and ran even faster than before, ran as hard as she could.

SMOKED

Her canteen slapped her butt as she ran, water sloshing, but Didi didn't care. All that mattered was this running. She opened up to full sprint, praying her dad hadn't already gotten to the other two men.

Through the western part of the forest, her paintball gun at the ready. Was it too obvious a place for Mr. Howard to be? But that was him all over, to go for the familiar and try to smoke her out. It's how Didi beat him in chess every time.

Slow down

No. Counterintuitive.

But slow down she did, listening for crashing in the brush. Nothing. Just birdsong and crab apples falling from branches.

A twig snapped.

Didi shot.

A deer.

It ran fast with its tail up, followed by another, Didi's red paint staining its side.

Goddammit!

Behind her—step speed fast, fast—

Mr. Howard in a crouch-run toward her through the trees.

keep ahead—!

Quick and low, Didi ran in her own crouch. *Stay in the lead! No paint, no yellow, not a shot at her back; no.*

Fast, fast, fast feet behind her—Mr. Howard was upright now, unfolding into a full run. Didi stretched her body up too and ran harder, faster, more—

"I'm on you, girl!" Mr. Howard yelled from behind.

Fly!

Didi flew faster than fast. Mr. Howard might have a longer stride, but his middle-aged belly was no match for her sprint. Up the hill for ten years, around the property for ten years—Didi could stay ahead of him.

She let him get nearer, though, nearer, near and then—

—took fast aim over her shoulder and fired.

Red.

"Damn!" Mr. Howard, dropping his paintball gun. "I thought I had you! Well done, Didi—you got me before—"

But Didi was already running hard, not hearing the rest. She knew, though. Before her dad.

Three red and just one man left, no paint on her at all. But what if her dad had started with Mr. Singleterry? The hardest first, not the easiest like she'd assumed?

don't think, don't think, don't think about that

Find Mr. Singleterry. Now. Before the sun flew any higher. He had the best shot of the four men, but if she had any luck, his shot would be sluggish like it sometimes was at the range—

Didi pulled her mind up short.

Just GO!

But where? Her dad's sprawling acres. There were still plenty of places for Mr. Singleterry to hide.

OPEN

Didi sprinted down the hill of the forest, scanning in all directions. The trees were thinning here, the forest nearly at an end.

She jittered to a stop at the fence at the edge of the woods and crouched down to study the valley beyond it. She was still shielded by the trees but would need to sneak forth if she wanted to fully scope out the area and plan.

She waited.

Then, cautiously, Didi stood and shielded her eyes with her hand against the watery glare of the late-morning sun. What was that? There? Right there in the middle of the valley?

Mr. Singleterry, standing right out in the open.

But *why?* Why, why, why, why? Was it a setup?

Didn't matter—

Not long to wonder.

"Didi," he cried as she came out of the trees. His paintball gun hung down useless in one hand. "Didi—this is all so intense—do you need me to talk to—"

No!

Fast and fiery like a fox, Didi charged at him. Got near enough to practically grab him by the belt and shot him point-blank, though she knew what that felt like, shot him in the thigh before he could utter another word.

Mr. Singleterry clutched at his leg and fell. No orange on him, though. What was this luck?

"Didi—"

luck? skill? do I got this for real?

None of their paint on me, I took down every one—

Relief almost made her buckle.

Oh God, thank you! I'm here! I'm alive!

But don't just stay here with Mr. Singleterry groaning—

Didi left her father's friend and ran straight ahead down the valley.

(I'm sorry, I'm sorry, I'm sorry—)

TOWARD

Didi stilled her feet and lay belly down in the valley grasses. She couldn't stay here long, but she needed time to think.

What was she supposed to do now?

Show my dad? No paint on my body? Only red on theirs?

All the men down. She got them all before him—

So find him, idiot! Let him see what you've done!

And what if he were still behind her, not knowing she'd won—would he be furious? Proud? Happy? Enraged?

Just find him! Show him! Then everything will be okay.

She won. She won. She got paint on the men.

Then I get—what?

A burger?

The sunshine?

Or just my own life?

But where was he?

Focus! Notice! Look in all directions!

Sunny. Dry now, even though Didi was slick with sweat. Cold like a knife in her chest.

Didi scoped carefully around.

There. What's that? Up there and over. Far away high, on top of the ridge.

Standing with his back to the valley, the well-trodden

slope behind him. In front of her dad would be his own house.

What?

But there was no turning back, only forward, right?

Those are the rules in chess for a pawn?

Which rules were which? What game was she playing? Oh God, please show her, please.

Go toward what scares you, never away

Plus I got all four men—! I did it! I won!

Didi skirted the edge of the valley and ran toward the bottom of the slope.

It was all grasses and sun, and her dad was focused southwest, the wind coming from in front of him. Didi stopped and was still.

Into the eerie of the valley came a scent from the south. Her father's sweat was in it but something stronger too, something sweet like a blossom, a locust tree blooming in spring.

This is almost winter—

Why was he just standing there?

Then Didi understood. During his own hunt for the men, he must have found each one already blasted with Didi's paint, down despite his ten-minute head start. Then, from up on the ridge, he'd seen her shoot Mr. Singleterry. So he was waiting. Waiting. Standing at the house because he knew she'd come back there in the end.

Didi quieted her breathing. Was this bad? Half bad? Not bad at all? Should she just stay here, be quiet and see?

But the wind revealed her by changing direction, blowing her own scent up the slope.

Her father spun round. Which gun was that in his hand?

"Get up here!" he shouted.

Frozen. But only for a split second. Didi ran automatically in answer to that voice. Up, up, up, the near-vertical incline feeling like nothing.

There he stood, trouble stick in his hands.

"I won," Didi stammered. "No paint. I got them. I won."

"'*I won*,'" he mimicked, eyes poison. "You stupid fuck. You think I care about that?"

Didi started, mind whirling. What was he saying? She'd done everything he told her! What did he mean he didn't care?

"But—"

"Shut up!" her dad yelled. "You haven't won! You've barely begun! Who gives a shit what was said at the house? I wanted the perfect opponent. Now I have it. You. And now it's *my* turn. You and me. Part two." He raised his rifle. "Run."

Didi ran.

Zig then zag, that's what they told you to do in elementary school if someone was after you, right? Only this wasn't an abduction; it was the opposite of that—

Don't let me die, not today, oh God, please, please, please

Didi jagged across the long front yard with its rocks and sticks tripping at her feet.

PAWN

Dead ahead was the house with its fence running behind. He was trapping her back to where they had begun. *Trade yourself in!* Hair wild and high with dirt and leaves from the hunt. *Be a queen! Be a knight! Or just a pawn that goes backward!*

"There's nowhere to go, Didi!" her father called behind her, and Didi slowed before the house, then walked, then stopped and turned.

Didi's dad faced her, rifle raised, his back to the ridge once more. Didi standing between him and the house, dirt drive with the locust trees to her left.

Didi lifted her hand.

"You dumb little shit," her father said. "How did you get that gun?"

BEFORE

(Ten minutes alone while he was gone for his head start. Didi was crouching down. The gun case was closed, locked electronically; what was she going to do?

Think! What would be his entry code?

ANDREW, she thought, but no. Too long. The spaces ran out after four.

"RIEV!" Of course. So she typed it: *R,* then *I, E* and then *V.*

Didi pulled uselessly at the lock.

Please!

What could it be if not his own name?

Then a word popped in her mind, and she knew she was right. The ass thought of himself as a:

KING.

K-I-N-G.

It worked. The door swung open, and there was the pistol, the one she slept with when he was gone. Didi tucked it into her tactical belt and breathed in, then out, then in again and stopped. One minute left to wait.

She sat down.)

HUNTER

The sun was high now, noon well past. But somewhere a hoot owl sounded.

"I MADE YOU!" he screamed across the yard. "You are nothing but what I created! You're a huntress, dammit, you're a *player*, you know how to win! I MADE YOU! Without me you'd be just some book-reading ass little kid!"

"I know," Didi said back. "You're a sculptor and you made me."

"That's right!" her dad shrieked. Then: "Fine! Keep the damn gun! Let's play equal! Play even! Play fair!"

Her father's rifle still aimed at Didi. Pistol still in her hand.

Eternity passed. Didi waiting, waiting. Birdsong sounding in the trees.

will we stand here with our arms up forever?

The light grew strange, blue and in waves, coming from the locust trees. It washed over her dad's face.

Blue, swirl, swirl, swirl.

what's going on? am I already dead?

Blue, pulse, pulse, pulse. Rifle in his hands.

"DROP THE GUN!"

Police shouting so loud, not at Didi but at him.

Mr. Singleterry was babbling. "He said it was ultimate

paintball. That's what he said! I didn't know! He said 'paint-ball guns provided'!"

"NOW!" bellowed one of the police, his voice in a mega-phone. "PUT THAT GUN DOWN!"

Trouble stick raised, pointed at Didi's heart. Her pistol still raised to meet it.

police closing in but not fast enough

Super Ball, Super Ball, bishop hitting king

"You ungrateful bitch!" her dad screamed. Then: "Fuck it!"

She watched his finger on the trigger, finger skeet watched.

He took his shot, spark blinking red, and Didi shot too, rapid-aim a hair left as she pulled the trigger on the pistol.

His bullet smashed, exploding in the air.

even as a cop shot clear at her dad.

But still he stood, ignoring his right arm, now pulsing blood. "I trained you," he said, upper lip lifted. "You were supposed to win the whole thing."

He turned and pointed his rifle at the cop.

"I did win, you bastard," she whispered as the police shot him in the chest. "And every chess game you ever won, I threw."

didi, are you all right

exchanged myself for a bishop
shot diagonally, not straight like
she'd trained
his shot's always to his right

didi, are you okay

"I called the police, Didi. It was all too weird!" Mr. Singleterry was sobbing by the police car. "All those years, all that hunting. The chess and this game. I was afraid he was going to kill you."

He was—

The police. "Didi, are you okay?"

A blanket draped around her shoulders, ambulance taking her dad.

"Am I arrested?" she cried.

"No, honey, no," the policewoman soothed her. "It's over and not your fault."

Wind picked up, blew the leaves from her hair. That scent again, locust tree blossoms in spring. Yet here it was, nearly the end of November.

"Come with us, honey."

"Is there anyone here we can call?"

"I'll take her!" cried Mr. Singleterry, sobbing, sobbing.

"NO!" screamed Didi. "Don't let any of them take me!"

"We won't, Didi, honey, no way."

"But is there anybody at all we could call?"

Didi shook her head, jamming her freezing hands into her pockets.

She started. Then she pulled a soft paper from one pocket of her camo.

Blue ink long faded and gone, years of palming it down. But it didn't matter. Didi had memorized that number when she was eight.

PART 6

AFTER

OPENING

Devin was twelve now, almost as tall as Didi. Didi looked down at short Lynn.

What happened? All the wrong sizes, and she shouldn't be here, taking up space in their home.

"This is your room, sweetie," Lynn said, gesturing. "Your bed with your comforter."

what did that mean?

comforter, comforter.

say it lots of times. It still doesn't make any sense.

"Oh, Didi," Lynn was crying. "Oh, my sweet, sweet girl."

This kept happening, Lynn crying, arms around Didi. Didi as stiff as a board. November was done, and Lynn and Devin had decorated for Christmas, Didi silent in the kitchen so as not to disturb them.

"Didi," Lynn said, "I have a question, and it's fine no matter how you answer." She drew a deep breath. "Do you want us to find your mom?"

"NO!" It was out of her mouth before she even thought. "I don't even know her name."

"The police can find it—"

"She left." Didi swallowed. Then, after a minute she said: "I wasn't worth it. Not enough for her to stay."

"You were," said Lynn. "You were worth it, Didi."

Was Lynn listening? "No. I just said. She left."

"Didi, listen to me. You were worth it. You are. You're a beautiful soul. You are worth the world as somebody's daughter."

Didi puffed a small puff through her nose. Her worth was over, finished for her, her dad being breathed for in a hospital.

Lynn was still talking. "You are worth everything," she said. "Honey, you are. You are more than what your father forced you to do."

How was she supposed to respond to that? But Devin was shouting: "The tree's tipping over!" And that was a good excuse to pretend she hadn't heard the words that poured over her like water.

Didi might be in a new state and town, but she read about her old school online. The kids from the chess club had picketed as they'd planned. They wore costumes for the picket line. It was surreal. There was Aiden on-screen, dressed as a pawn. Dallin as a fabulous rook, crenellations as a crown on his forehead. Pascal was a chessboard and Lexie was a timer. Those two stood next to each other. Didi wondered if they were going out.

The picketing had worked too. Donations poured in and

the team went to states. They lost, but that was whatever. It was the going that counted for them.

What would I have been if I had been there for the picket line? Didi wondered. Then she shook her head. Of course she wouldn't have joined in.

But if she had, she would've dressed in collared shirt and jeans. Like the coach. Like Nomura. The one who took care of the team.

"My dad'll come!"

"No, he won't!"

"Yes, he will! You don't know!"

"You're safe here, honey! I promise!"

only right on this bed. only right here. right now. only in this one second.

Lynn went over and over the statistics with her.

"I wouldn't have taken you in if I thought it was a danger. He has no idea where you live."

"He'll find out!" Didi cried.

"No," Lynn repeated for the zillionth time. "You can use my last name now. Oh, sweet girl, let me make it official."

yes

but Didi swallowed the word and her want.

"Didi. Listen. You didn't win the parent lottery. But I won the one for a new daughter."

She hugged Didi again, and Didi felt her arms lift stiff and up, before they dropped back down to her sides.

"he'll come!"
"no, he won't!"
"yes, he will! you don't know!"

"He's in the prison hospital, and he can't even move, Diana," said the policeman that Lynn got to come over. "He'll be in jail for years. And you'll always have a restraining order."

"That's only three hundred feet or one hundred yards. That's not enough room. A gun could cut through that in a second."

"It would have to be a military grade weapon."

No comfort there because who knew what he'd stashed.

"If he ever gets out," the policeman continued, "which he won't, because he's nearly vegetative, there's very little chance he could shoot again. Not with the wound he sustained to his right arm."

But Didi knew he would practice with his left. Practice until he could come for her. She couldn't feel any peace.

Her thoughts were a torrent, threatening to overtake her.
He loved me! He said so!
(Her dad had never cared about her
Only that she belonged to him)
He loved me! He said so!
(She wasn't even a person to him

She was a thing)

(He'd thingified her! How could you do that to someone?
Especially somebody you love?)

You're not allowed to make a person a thing.

Forget her mother having left her father—

What kind of person would leave a three-year-old with that man?

Didi didn't want to know.

She would never try to find her mother or even think about
her again.

New year. New school in this new town. Didi wanted to hide
in a cave. But no one seemed to connect her to all that news
coverage. She was Diana the New One today, and that was it.

Lunch. Didi went through the line.

I'll find a table by myself.

"Diana!" Who was that? Some girl from her lit class. "Come
sit with us. Let us tell you what the deal is."

Didi took a deep breath in and breathed out.

*Can I get there by half steps? If I do a step, then its half, then one
smaller and more? I can never get to that table.*

Shut up. Zeno's paradox was bullshit.

Just walk, like normal. Teenager steps.

Then she was there and sat down.

Little rabbit in the wood,
Little lass by the window stood,
Saw the rabbit running by
Knocking at her door.
"'Help me, help me, help!' she said.
"'Ere the huntsman shoots me dead!'
"'Come, little rabbit, come with me!
"'Safely you shall be.'"

ACKNOWLEDGMENTS

These people I thank with all my heart and a fervent, perhaps even off-putting intensity: Alan. Tobin. Adrienne. My SiS. Especially Melody. Jen. Jane. Andrea. Poopaw. Martha. Cupcake shops. Coffee shops. High schools. And Caitlyn and Linda, the wonder team.